Promises are made to be broken

"Becka, I need your help," Cat Morgan said to her sister as they headed down the hall. "Marla's been nominated for Winter Carnival Princess, and I promised her I'd help her get elected."

"Fine," Becka said. "*If* you help me with Michelle."

"It's a deal," said Cat. Then she stopped still. Taped to her locker was a plain white envelope – an envelope she recognized.

Her heart pounding, Cat ripped it off her locker and tore it open. Becka read it over her shoulder.

"To Catherine Morgan. From the Student Council. It is our great pleasure to inform you that you have been selected as a nominee for Winter Carnival Princess."

Cat read the line over and over. A tingle started in her toes and shot all the way through her entire body. Winter Carnival Princess. Princess Cat. She was dizzy, she was floating, she was riding on a cloud.

She turned to Becka in ecstasy. But Becka's words brought Cat back down to earth with a thud.

"Well, well. Still want me to help get votes for Marla? You know Marla – your best friend?"

Titles by Marilyn Kaye available in Lions

THREE OF A KIND

1 With Friends Like These, Who Needs Enemies?
2 Home's a Nice Place to Visit, But I Wouldn't Want to
Live There
3 Will the Real Becka Morgan Please Stand Up?
4 Two's Company, Four's a Crowd
5 Cat Morgan, Working Girl
6 101 Ways to Win Homecoming Queen

SISTERS

Phoebe
Daphne
Cassie
Lydia

A Friend Like Phoebe

101 Ways to Win Homecoming Queen

Marilyn Kaye

Lions
An Imprint of HarperCollins*Publishers*

For Moira Longino

First published in the U.S. in 1991
by Harper Paperbacks,
a division of HarperCollins*Publishers*

First published in the U.K. in 1992 in Lions

Lions is an imprint of
HarperCollins Children's Books,
a division of HarperCollins*Publishers*
77-85 Fulham Palace Road,
Hammersmith, London W6 8JB

Printed and bound in Great Britain by
HarperCollinsManufacturing Glasgow

One

Becka Morgan shivered. The cold wind outside seemed to be coming in through the walls of the old farmhouse.

"Cat! Come on, let's go!" Becka pulled on her parka and fumbled with the zip. When there was no response to her call, she tried again. "Cat!"

A voice drifted out from the kitchen at the other end of the house. "Just a minute!"

Becka glanced at the clock on the mantel over the fireplace and tapped her foot impatiently. "What is she doing, anyway?"

Josie Morgan uttered a snort. "Three guesses, and the first two don't count. Talking on the phone, what else?" Josie grabbed a faded knitted cap from the coat-rack and tugged it down over her short, unruly red hair. Then she flung a scarf around her shoulders.

Annie Morgan joined them in the living room. "Ben will be down in a minute," she said. "Are you all ready to go?"

"*We're* ready," Becka said. "But Cat's still on the phone."

"Cat!" Annie called.

"In a second," the voice floated back.

"Becka, put your hood up," Annie said.

Carefully, Becka tucked her long blonde hair under the hood of her coat. At least there was one benefit from the cold weather – her hair didn't frizz like it did in the summer.

Annie took a long woollen scarf from the coatrack and wrapped it around Becka's neck. It wasn't very comfortable, but Becka didn't object to her fussing. There was something nice and cozy about Annie's concern. Even after eight months, Becka still got a special pleasure from having a mother who cared.

"You, too, Josie," Annie ordered. "That scarf won't serve any purpose just hanging there." She beckoned Josie closer and tied it tighter. "I don't want you girls getting the flu."

"I'm never ill," Josie replied. She crooked her arm and flexed a muscle, which wasn't very impressive under her bulky jacket. "I'm an athlete."

Ben Morgan entered the room just in time to catch that announcement. "No one's arguing

6

that. Not after your performance last night on the basketball court."

Josie flushed slightly, but Becka could see the glow of pride in her eyes. "That was pure luck, making that basket in the last second."

"I don't call it luck," Ben replied. "I call it talent. I'll bet those boys are pretty happy they let a girl in the team."

Josie pulled the scarf over her mouth, and her voice was muffled. "Yeah, I guess."

The room was getting warmer, and Becka was beginning to feel stifled by her wrappings. Again, she looked at the clock. "We have to go."

Ben put on his jacket. "Okay, I'm ready." Then he scratched his head and turned to Annie. "Wait a minute. I may be mistaken, but don't we have three daughters?"

"You forget," Annie said. "One of them happens to be permanently attached to a telephone. Cat!"

"Coming!"

"Annie, do something," Becka pleaded. "She's going to make us late."

"Well, it may require surgery to separate her ear from the phone, but I'll see what I can do." Annie headed back towards the kitchen.

Becka started chewing on a fingernail, and Josie eyed her with scorn. "Don't be so jittery. We'll get there."

7

"But I want us to be there on time," Becka said. She fished the invitation out of her pocket and read aloud: "'On Sunday, February fifth, Willoughby Hall will celebrate its fiftieth year of caring for homeless children. You are cordially invited to join us for a reception and tour at two o'clock.'"

"I think we can pass up the tour," Josie said.

Becka nodded. They knew every nook and cranny of the building – after all, they'd lived there for thirteen years. "But I don't want to miss the reception. I'll bet Mrs. Parker's whipped up all kinds of fabulous goodies."

"Here's the missing daughter," Annie announced, with Cat in tow. Despite her annoyance, Becka couldn't help being impressed with the way Cat looked. Her thick, glossy black hair bounced on the shoulders of her pale green sweater, and her smooth complexion was highlighted by just a touch of make-up.

"Then we're all set," Ben said. He slapped his trouser pocket. "Uh-oh, I left the car keys upstairs. Be right back." He turned and took the stairs two at a time.

"It's about time," Becka told Cat sternly. Cat didn't look the tiniest bit apologetic, but at least she had the courtesy to pretend she was.

8

"Sorry, you guys. But I couldn't get off the phone. It was something serious." Cat slipped into her white fake-fur coat, lifting her hair so it flowed down the back.

"Who were you talking to?" Josie asked.

"Marla."

Becka and Josie exchanged looks. Cat was making the phone call sound like something out of the ordinary, even though Cat talked to her best friend every day.

"Is something wrong with Marla?" Annie asked.

Cat nodded solemnly. "She's got such awful problems. It's so bad. Truly devastating, even."

Becka's eyes widened. "Oh no! What happened to her?"

Cat explained. "There's this boy she really likes, Steve Garner. She finally got him to ask her out for last night. And he stood her up. Can you believe it? Marla could hardly get out of bed this morning, and I don't blame her."

"Is that all?" Josie rolled her eyes. "For crying out loud, Cat, you make that sound like a tragedy."

"Well, it *is*," Cat insisted. "At least, *most* girls would think so. Most *normal* girls."

"Thank goodness I'm not like most girls," Josie muttered. "And for your information, I *am* normal."

9

"That's a matter of opinion," Cat snapped.

"Girls," Annie said automatically. "Don't squabble."

"Annie!" Ben's plaintive voice came from upstairs. "I can't find the keys!"

"He's probably looking straight at them," Annie murmured, and went up the stairs. Becka turned to the other girls. "She's right. We shouldn't squabble, especially not today."

"Why especially not today?" Josie asked.

"Because we're going to Willoughby Hall. And for the first time, we won't be there as poor, pitiful orphans. We're going as sisters. We're the Morgan girls now." She smiled blissfully.

Cat and Josie exchanged amused looks. "Watch out," Josie warned Cat. "She's getting mushy."

"Yeah," Cat agreed. "She probably wants us to skip into Willoughby Hall holding hands." Josie choked back her laughter.

Becka sighed. It was no use expecting them to understand how meaningful this day was to her. But it wasn't that long ago that they'd been three unrelated orphans, with absolutely nothing in common except for their age, thirteen, and the fact that they shared a room in Willoughby Hall. They'd all dreamed of someday having parents and a real home, but none honestly believed it would ever happen.

10

After all, most prospective parents wanted cute little babies, not big thirteen-year-old girls. Who could have ever imagined that people like Annie and Ben Morgan would appear and decide to adopt all three of them?

To Becka, it was a beautiful miracle, something that happened only in stories. Her heart fluttered and she still got misty-eyed when she thought of this amazing turn of events. And today they were returning to the orphanage as a family of sisters. What an inspiration they'd be to the lonely orphans who thought they'd never be adopted! They'd prove to the kids that miracles do happen. The Morgan sisters would give them hope.

Annie came back downstairs, and Ben followed, waving the keys in triumph. "Okay, we're off."

Annie made some last-minute adjustments to their scarves, hats, and coats. "Put on your gloves," she said as she hugged and kissed each girl. "And have a wonderful time."

To Becka, Annie's embrace seemed a little tighter than usual. Maybe she was afraid they'd have such a wonderful time seeing their old friends that they'd want to stay there. After all, eight months ago, Josie had run away and gone to Willoughby Hall. But she was only gone less than one day. Becka

11

wanted to assure Annie that that would never happen again, but her sisters would just laugh at her. Sure, there had been good times at Willoughby Hall. But nothing compared with having a real home. Even Josie thought so now.

The girls hurried to the car, and Becka and Josie climbed into the back seat. Cat sat up front with Ben. As he started the engine, she turned around and frowned. "Josie, this thing at Willoughby Hall is a big deal. Did you have to wear jeans?"

"Of course I did," Josie replied. "Otherwise no one would have recognized me."

"Ben, what time is it?" Becka asked.

"Quarter after one," Ben murmured. He never talked much in the car, because he concentrated on his driving.

"I hope we're not going to be too late," Becka said. Willoughby Hall was almost an hour away.

Josie grinned. "What's the matter? Afraid we'll get demerits?"

That remark brought a smile to Becka's face. She thought about all the demerits she'd gathered at Willoughby Hall, for being late to meals or forgetting a chore. That was another benefit of adoption. Ben and Annie might scold, but they didn't hand out demerits.

"It's cool to be a little late for social events," Cat remarked. "That way, you can make an entrance."

"Yeah, I can picture you now," Josie said. "'Hello, you poor little orphans. *I've* been adopted.'"

Ben had stopped at a red light and actually heard that remark. "Cat wouldn't do that," he said. "You know, there are a lot of kids at Willoughby Hall who'd give anything to have a home. You don't want to show off in front of them."

Becka was glad he couldn't see her smile. Josie's description of the way Cat would act sounded pretty accurate to her.

She'd never behave that way. She remembered all too well her own loneliness when she was an orphan. She remembered the envy she used to feel when kids at school talked about their parents, how she got choked up when she watched TV shows about families. She recalled the day she left Willoughby Hall, and the wistful expressions on the faces of her fellow orphans. She'd *never* brag about her own good fortune to them.

She turned to Josie. "I'll bet you can't wait to see Mrs. Parker." Josie had been very close to the orphanage cook.

Josie nodded. "Yeah, I've got a lot to tell her about."

"Wait till she hears you've become the star of the Green Falls Junior High basketball team," Becka said with a smile.

Josie's smile faded. She turned away and looked out of the window.

Becka gazed at her curiously. It seemed like, lately, every time the subject of basketball came up, Josie looked weird. Becka couldn't figure out why. What Ben had said before was absolutely true. Josie was becoming *the* person to watch during the basketball games – and not just because she was the only girl on the team. Becka didn't know much about basketball, but even she could tell that Josie was good, better than most of the boys.

As they drew closer to the orphanage and familiar sights came into view, Becka felt her pulse quicken. "There's our old school," she said. "And there's the library." Then, like the others, she lapsed into silence. She wondered if they were thinking what she was thinking: What would it be like, going back?

Becka leaned through the window to kiss Ben goodbye, while Cat proceeded sedately towards the entrance. Josie raced past both of them. She pushed open the door, and then stood stock-still in the hallway.

Hanging from the ceiling was a huge banner

that read WELCOME. Colourful streamers and clusters of balloons decorated the walls. From her position, Josie could see into the television room, where groups of children and adults stood around tables laden with food.

Cat and Becka came in behind her. "Wow, look at this place!" Becka exclaimed.

"No kidding," Cat breathed. "Check out the new rug. And the walls!"

Josie hadn't even noticed those things. But on closer examination, she saw that the old threadbare carpet had been replaced by a beautiful rug, and the faded, peeling wallpaper she remembered was gone.

"This place has really been fixed up," Cat said.

"And it's about time, right?" Mrs. Scanlon approached them, smiling. "Welcome, girls! I'm so glad you could come."

As the girls greeted the orphanage's director, Josie found herself hiding her hands behind her back. Then, realizing what she was doing, she almost laughed out loud. When she had lived here, she had always hidden her hands when she ran into Mrs. Scanlon, for fear the director would spot her dirty fingernails and give her a demerit.

"How do you like our improvements?" Mrs. Scanlon asked.

"Oh, it's just lovely," Cat said in that gushy voice that always got on Josie's nerves.

"We've been very fortunate," the director told them. "We've received generous contributions this year." She gestured towards the television room. "Some of our benefactors are here. Why don't you come in and meet them?"

Cat and Becka started forward, but Josie hung back. "Uh, Mrs. Scanlon, could I go see Mrs. Parker first?"

"Of course, dear. I think you know where to find her."

Josie had a pretty solid idea. She took off down the hall and burst into the kitchen.

The plump, gray-haired woman was bent over a large pot, her face red from the steam. When she saw Josie, she replaced the lid on the pot, wiped her hands on her apron, and threw her arms around her.

"Josie, it's wonderful to see you!"

Before Josie could say the same to her, a girl appeared at the door. "Mrs. Scanlon says we need more spinach dip, please."

Mrs. Parker released Josie, went to the refrigerator, and pulled out a bowl. "Here you are, Trixie." Then she hurried to the stove and checked on something cooking inside. "Whew, what a day!"

"Can I help?" Josie asked.

16

"Oh no, honey. You're a guest here today."

"That's okay. I can just pretend I'm an orphan." With that, she picked up a carrot from a stack. "Toss me a peeler."

It was like old times, working side by side with Mrs. Parker.

"Now, tell me what's going on," the cook demanded. "Are you happy now with your new home?"

"It doesn't even feel new anymore," Josie said. "Annie and Ben are terrific. It's like they've been my parents forever."

"What about Becka and Cat? Are you girls getting along?"

"Mmm . . . yes and no. Mostly yes, I guess."

Mrs. Parker nodded. "Just like regular sisters. What about school?"

"Well, classes are boring and the cafeteria food's really awful, but . . . I'm on the basketball team."

"How exciting!" Mrs. Parker lifted the lid on the pot and tasted whatever it was inside. "This needs something . . . " She added some spices and then turned back to Josie. "Now, what were you saying about basketball?"

"I scored twenty points in the last game."

Mrs. Parker pulled a tray of cookies from the oven and began arranging them on a platter. "Wonderful! That must make you pretty popular with the rest of the team."

Josie gave her carrot a fierce swipe. "Huh," she muttered.

Her tone got Mrs. Parker's full attention. She sat down at the table and faced Josie. "Okay, what's the problem?"

Josie shifted in her seat. It would be such a relief to tell someone her worries. "I'm not sure. See, I'm the only girl on the team . . ."

The cook frowned. "Don't tell me the boys are sexist."

"I don't *think* so," Josie replied. "I mean, they're not nasty or anything like that. I just don't feel like I'm really part of the team. Like, they don't accept me."

The girl who had come for the dip reappeared at the door. "Mrs. Scanlon says we'll need some more punch pretty soon."

"All right, Trixie, I'll bring it in." Shaking her head wearily, Mrs. Parker went to the refrigerator. "I'm glad we don't have a fiftieth anniversary every year."

"Got any good advice for me?" Josie asked hopefully.

"What, dear?"

"About the basketball team. How can I get the boys to accept me?"

"Oh, Josie, you worry too much," Mrs.

18

Parker said. "You just play the best possible game you can play, and they'll love you!"

Josie nodded. "Yeah, I'll try." But deep inside she knew it wouldn't be that easy.

"That was a lovely reception," Cat told Ellen Perry, one of the counsellors. Ellen was taking the girls through the building, pointing out all the improvements and renovations.

"Great food," Josie remarked.

Becka agreed. "That's one thing I really miss about Willoughby Hall. The food."

Ellen's eyebrows rose. "Don't your parents feed you well?"

Josie laughed. "*I* feed them better. Ben and Annie aren't exactly great cooks. But I'm training them."

"They're great in every other way, though," Becka added.

"You're very lucky girls," Ellen said. "Let me show you how we've fixed up your old room. You won't even recognize it!" She opened the door. "Oh! I'm sorry, Michelle. I thought all you kids were downstairs."

The small, slight girl with short fair hair looked up from her book. "I just felt like reading."

"Well, we won't disturb you," Ellen said. "I'll show our guests the room next door."

Cat and Josie followed her, but Becka

19

lingered. "This used to be my old room," she told the girl sitting on the bed.

The girl smiled shyly. "Does it look very different?"

Becka remembered sickly green walls and crooked blinds at the windows. Now there were real curtains, bright flowered wallpaper, and dressers that weren't chipped or scratched. "It's a lot nicer now. I'm Becka. What's your name?"

"Michelle Jones."

"How old are you?"

"Nine. Almost ten," she added quickly.

Becka smiled. She remembered how she herself always used to say she was "almost" a year older than she was. "How long have you been at Willoughby Hall?"

"Three months."

Then she must have just lost her parents recently, Becka thought. She gazed at the younger girl in sympathy.

Michelle must have read her mind. "I was living at another orphanage and it closed, so I was sent here. My parents died when I was a baby. At least, I guess they did."

"What do you mean?"

Michelle went a little pink. "Well . . . actually, I was, uh, abandoned. They left me in the emergency room of a hospital. I don't even know who my parents were."

20

Becka's mouth fell open. "I was abandoned, too!"

"Really?"

Becka nodded. "Someone – maybe my mother, I don't know – left me on the doorstep here at Willoughby Hall. There was a note saying my name was Becka, but that was all. The people here gave me the last name Blue, because that was the colour of the blanket I was wrapped in. How did you get your last name?"

"I guess someone at the hospital just made it up," Michelle said. "Jones. Whoever made it up didn't have much imagination! Becka Blue . . . now, that's a pretty name."

"Actually, Blue's not my last name anymore," Becka told her. "It's Becka Morgan now. I was adopted."

Michelle's eyes widened. "You were? When?"

"Just eight months ago."

"Wow," Michelle murmured. "The kids here say no one over eight ever gets adopted."

"That's not always true," Becka stated. "Josie and Cat and I are the proof."

"Who are Josie and Cat?"

"The girls who are with me. The Morgans adopted them, too."

"Wow," Michelle said again. She looked at Becka with interest.

"I hope I'm not disturbing your reading,"

21

Becka said. "I read a lot, too, and I don't like people bothering me when I've got a good book."

"It's okay," Michelle said, sticking a bookmark in the book and closing it. Becka sat down on the edge of her bed.

"What are you reading?"

"*Jane Eyre*. Have you ever read it?"

"Have I!" Becka exclaimed. "It's one of my all-time favourites. I've read it at least five times!"

A smile lit up Michelle's face. "Isn't it wonderful?"

"Absolutely," Becka said. "I cried when she was sent away to that awful orphanage."

"Me, too," Michelle agreed. "I guess there are worse places than Willoughby Hall."

"Don't you like it here?" Becka asked.

Michelle's smile disappeared. "Oh sure, everyone's nice and all, but . . . "

"But what?"

"It's still an orphanage. It must be wonderful to have a family and a home." She looked at Becka eagerly. "Tell me what it's like."

"It's . . . nice," Becka said.

Michelle persisted. "What's your house like? And your parents, how do they act? Do you have any pets?"

Becka tried to answer each question without bragging or making her life sound too much better than Michelle's. But as hard as she tried, she could still see Michelle's eyes getting shiny and wistful.

In a strange way, she felt like she'd seen this girl before. She realized that, in a way, she *had*. In a mirror. Talking to Michelle was like talking to a younger version of herself. It made the longing in Michelle's face even harder to bear.

"Becka? Where are you?" Josie's voice rang out in the hall.

"I'm coming," Becka called back. "It was nice meeting you, Michelle."

"Maybe I'll see you again sometime," the girl said.

"I hope so." Becka got up and headed for the door. She could feel Michelle's eyes on her as she left the room.

Two

Cat could see the gloom written all over Marla's face, even from the other side of the room. All during French class, she'd been wanting to pass Marla a note, telling her not to feel so bad about that idiot Steve Garner. But Mademoiselle Casalls never took her eyes off the class, and Cat couldn't take the risk of getting caught.

As soon as the bell rang, Cat snatched up her books and manoeuvered through the other students to reach Marla. "Cheer up," she ordered her best friend. "Steve Garner is a jerk."

Marla nodded, but she didn't smile. "I saw him this morning. He told me he forgot we had a date. If that's true, he's pretty dumb. And if it's not . . ."

"Then he's even dumber," Cat finished. "Personally, I don't know what you ever saw

24

in him. He's short, he doesn't play sports, and he's not even all that cute."

"Yeah, you're right," Marla acknowledged. "I guess it was just a silly crush. I'm just bugged that he didn't even bother to call. I feel stupid."

"I know. But it's not the end of the world. Don't let yourself get too upset over this."

"That's easy for you to say," Marla sighed. "I'll bet you've never been stood up."

In all honesty, Cat had to admit that was true. Actually, she couldn't imagine anything so totally humiliating ever happening to her. But that didn't mean she couldn't feel sincerely sorry for Marla.

The girls walked slowly down the hall towards the gym. Cat was in no hurry to get to the physical education class, and Marla was dragging her feet. Cat watched her uneasily. It wasn't like Marla to get depressed. She was usually so cheerful and self-confident, always available to listen to Cat's woes. Cat couldn't count the number of times Marla had lent an ear to her troubles and complaints. Marla always offered good, solid advice about boy problems, sister problems, money problems. Cat knew it was *her* turn now to be a helpful friend. But she wasn't quite sure she knew how to play this role.

"You don't need Steve Garner," she began. "There are other guys around."

"Yeah, yeah, I know. It just feels like nothing's going right for me lately. First, I put my favorite sweater in the washing machine and it shrunk. Then Steve blew me off. And to top it all off, I got a C in that French test we got back today." She let out another deep sigh. "I guess that's what they call the straw that broke the camel's back."

"I didn't do very well either," Cat assured her. "B minus." She tried to think of a way to change the subject and get Marla's mind off her problems. "Honestly, you'd think getting married would make Mademoiselle Casalls lighten up. It seems to me like she's getting tougher."

"Maybe she and her husband aren't getting along," Marla suggested.

"Are you kidding? Have you ever seen her husband? He's *gorgeous*."

Marla's voice dropped. "Speaking of gorgeous, don't look now, but Todd's staring at you."

Cat caught a glimpse of him out of the corner of her eye. Her ex-boyfriend was leaning against a wall, talking with a couple of other guys. But his eyes were definitely on her. She sniffed. "He's been looking at me like that ever since he broke up with Heather."

"He still likes you," Marla murmured.

"Too bad," Cat replied. "There's no way I'd ever be interested in one of Heather Beaumont's rejects."

"You used to like him," Marla said.

Cat didn't need reminding. "That was different." She smiled at the memory. It had been fun, luring Todd away from Heather when Cat had first moved to Green Falls. And for a while, she'd been satisfied with the relationship. Todd was cute, athletic, and popular. Too bad he was also boring.

"Of course, I suppose you don't need Todd," Marla said. "Now that you've got Bailey."

There was a slight note of envy in her voice, and Cat couldn't blame her. With his California-surfer good looks and sense of humour, Bailey was definitely a major improvement over Todd. Cat marvelled at her own good fortune in attracting him. Yes, she was lucky. Not like poor Marla. She felt a surge of sympathy. What could she say to cheer up her friend?

She did know one sure-fire method, and she gave it a shot. "Want to go shopping after school today? I could get out of working at the store, and there's a sale at the Town Shoppe."

"I can't," Marla said with regret. "I'm

on the planning committee for the Winter Carnival, and we've got a meeting today right after school."

"What's this Winter Carnival thing anyway?" Cat asked. "I keep hearing people talk about it."

Marla shrugged. "Oh, just lots of activities. Ice skating, skiing, that sort of thing. There's the big basketball game with Easton High, and a dance."

It all sounded like fun to Cat, but Marla wasn't showing any enthusiasm at all. "That's something to look forward to," Cat said encouragingly.

"I'll be lucky if I even get a date," Marla mumbled.

They entered the noisy locker room, packed with girls changing into shorts for class. Cat's eyes went to a sign on the wall that hadn't been there the day before. It read, CHEERLEADER TRYOUTS, TODAY, 3.30 P.M., GYM.

"Why are they having cheerleader tryouts in the middle of the semester?" Cat asked.

Trisha Heller, sitting on a bench nearby, answered her. "One of the cheerleaders got kicked off because her grade average dropped."

"Heather Beaumont?" Cat asked hopefully.

Trisha grinned. "Unfortunately, no. Some other girl."

"Oh." Cat had always admired the cheerleaders, in their adorable short skirts, kicking and leaping and doing cartwheels, with the eyes of the entire student body on them. And Heather Beaumont, Cat's sworn enemy, was captain.

Well, Cat could kick and leap and turn a cartwheel. And she'd look great in one of those short skirts. She could just imagine Heather's reaction – she'd have a fit if Cat became a cheerleader. What a pleasant thought. Cat studied the sign again and made a mental note of the time and place.

"I think I'll try out," Marla said.

Cat looked at her in surprise. Marla had never shown any interest in cheerleading before, although Cat knew that she had run for pep club vice-president last year. "Why?"

"I don't know. It might cheer me up. If I get chosen, that is." She pulled a pencil from her bag and jotted down the time and place on her notebook. "I hope there's not too much competition."

Cat smiled thinly. She mentally erased the time and place from her mind.

★   ★   ★

Josie stood with her knees slightly bent, her hands on her knees, and her eyes on the basketball in Alex Hayes's hands. She tried to block out the sound of the girls jumping up and down and cheering on the other side of the gym. This was an important play that they were practicing for the first time, and she had to concentrate.

According to the strategy Coach Meadows had laid out for them, Alex would pretend he was about to throw the ball to the player on his left, then quickly turn and toss it right, to Todd. Todd was supposed to aim toward the basketball hoop, then shoot the ball to Josie, who was closer to the hoop. Hopefully, the guy from the other team who was blocking Josie would be looking at the hoop instead of at the ball, and Josie would have a clear shot at the basket.

Alex faked his throw and got the ball to Todd. Todd pretended he was about to try for the hoop, then threw the ball toward Josie. Josie ran forward to get it. But suddenly, Gary Cole darted in front of her and grabbed it.

The shrill sound of Coach Meadows's whistle filled the air. Everyone froze and waited while the large man stalked out onto the floor. His expression was fierce.

"What was that about?" he barked. "Murphy, can't you remember a simple instruction? That ball was supposed to go to Morgan."

Todd scratched his head. "Yeah, Coach, I know. But – "

Gary Cole spoke up. "She wasn't paying attention, Coach. She didn't even see it coming. I figured if that's what she does during a real game, I'd better be prepared to catch it myself, since I'm closest to her."

Josie glared at him. "What are you talking about? I saw it coming! I was heading straight for it when you – "

A short blast from the coach's whistle silenced her. "Cut it out!" he bellowed. "I don't want any arguments. Now, we've got a big game coming up on Saturday. We haven't been able to beat Sweetwater in two years, and I want that record broken. So let's see a little teamwork here. You got that?" He gave them his standard threatening look.

There was a general bobbing of heads among the players. The coach turned to Josie. "That was a nice shot you made earlier. Keep it up."

Josie beamed and murmured, "Thanks, Coach."

"Okay, hit the showers! Murphy, I want to talk to you." Todd, the captain of the team, scooped up the ball, tucked it under his arm, and followed Coach Meadows to the benches. The other boys, laughing and talking and slapping each other on the back, headed towards the door leading to their locker room. As Gary Cole passed Josie, she called out to him, but he hurried by as if he hadn't heard her.

What was that all about? she wondered. She'd never paid much attention to Gary before, except to notice that he was probably the weakest member of the team. When they practised hoops, he hardly ever got the ball in. He had short arms and short legs, and the coach never put him in crucial positions. Luckily, the other guys liked Gary and didn't make fun of his lack of talent. Josie didn't understand why Gary had snatched that ball away from her. What was he trying to prove?

She started toward the girls' locker room, but then she noticed that Todd had finished his conversation with the coach. She backtracked and hurried over to him before he could enter the boys' locker room.

"Listen, Todd, I wasn't daydreaming or anything on the court. Gary jumped right in front of me. You must have seen him do that."

Todd looked distinctly uncomfortable. He bounced the ball a couple of times. "I wasn't really watching."

Josie stared at him in bewilderment. Of course he'd been watching! He'd been the one throwing the ball! Todd started edging backward, as if he was trying to get away from her. Josie tried to remember what Mrs. Parker had told her. *Just play the best possible game you can play, and the guys will love you.* She didn't want their love. A little acceptance would be enough. And it looked like she wasn't even going to get that. "Wait a second, Todd."

With a show of reluctance, Todd stopped moving, but his eyes didn't meet hers. "Yeah?"

"How am I doing?"

He shrugged. "Okay. You heard what the coach said."

Why couldn't he grin and slap her on the back, like the guys did with each other? Josie gave up. "Thanks." She turned to go to her locker room.

"Hey, Josie . . . "

Eagerly, she whirled around. "Yeah?"

"Um . . . how's Cat doing?"

Josie didn't let her disappointment show. "She's fine."

"Still going out with that Hudson guy?"

"I guess. I don't keep her social calendar."

Just then, Gary Cole stuck his head out the door. "Hey, Murphy, hurry up. We're all going to the bowling alley."

Todd brightened. "Right, I'm coming." He disappeared into the locker room. Josie waited a minute, hoping that the invitation to the

33

bowling alley might be extended to her. She smiled brightly at Gary, trying to show him that she didn't hold a grudge about his move on the court.

His only response was a sneer. Then he pointed to the sign by the door. "Boys only," he stated, as if she couldn't read. As if she was about to walk in there!

Or maybe he was referring to their bowling plans. With as much dignity as she could muster, Josie turned and walked away.

At Morgan's Country Foods, there was a momentary lull between customers. Annie pushed a wisp of hair out of her eyes. "What an afternoon! I don't know how we would have managed without you girls here."

Becka could believe that. Ever since she and Cat had arrived from school, they'd been waiting on customers while Annie handled the cash register and Ben unpacked some crates. They had Becka to thank for the recent upswing in business. Because Becka had miss-stated an ad about the store, then had to retract it, the store had got some publicity. Now they were busy almost every day.

"You two must be beat," Ben said. "As soon as Josie gets back, you can take a break."

"Here she comes now," Cat announced,

peering out of the window. She immediately reached under the counter and started putting on her gloves. *So typical*, Becka thought. Cat wouldn't stay a minute more than necessary.

"How was practice?" Ben asked as Josie pulled off her jacket.

"Okay," Josie replied. "But we couldn't use the whole court because of the dumb cheerleaders."

"Did you see Marla with them?" Cat asked.

Josie shook her head. "I had more important things to do than watch girls acting goofy."

"I didn't know Marla was a cheerleader," Annie remarked.

"She's not, yet," Cat told her. "But there's an opening on the squad, so she's trying out."

"Good grief, why?" Josie asked. "I thought Marla had some brains. Cheerleading is so stupid."

"Are you crazy?" Cat screeched. "Cheerleading's only about the coolest thing you can do."

Becka eyed her curiously. "If you feel that way about it, how come you're not trying out?"

"I was going to," Cat admitted. "But when Marla said *she* wanted to try out, I decided I'd better not. She's been pretty down lately. I'd hate for her to have another disappointment."

"Honestly, Cat, you're so conceited," Josie said. "You act like you're positively sure you would have beaten her for the place."

"Well, excuse me," Cat said in an offended voice. She turned to Annie. "Honestly, you try to do something nice for a person and some people can't deal with it."

Annie spoke soothingly. "I think what you did was very noble. Making a sacrifice for a friend isn't easy, but I'll bet you feel good about it."

Cat preened. Josie started coughing loudly, like she was trying to cover up a laugh. Becka had a hard time choking back a giggle, too. Making *any* kind of sacrifice for *any*one wasn't exactly Cat's style.

Cat shot them both a dirty look. "I guess you guys don't understand what it's like to be unselfish for a change."

It was getting impossible for Becka to hold back the laughter that was rising in her throat. Cat, a noble and unselfish person. Accepting that would take a major mental readjustment!

A jingle over the door ended the conversation. "Customers," Annie said unnecessarily. They all turned towards the front of the store with their fixed welcoming smiles. But those forced expressions dissolved when they saw who the customers were.

36

"Mrs. Parker!" Josie shrieked. "What are *you* doing here?"

The cook embraced Josie, Becka, and Cat, and shook hands with Annie and Ben.

"It's lovely to see you," Annie exclaimed. In the general chorus of greetings, no one seemed to notice the girl huddling at Mrs. Parker's side. Except Becka.

"Michelle, hi! Remember me?"

Michelle smiled shyly, nodded, and looked around the store. "Do you work here?"

"We all do," Becka said. "It's a family business." She turned to the others. "Hey, everyone, this is Michelle." She introduced the girl to Annie and Ben.

"This isn't just a social visit," Mrs. Parker told them. "Word has it you folks have the best jams and jellies around. How would you like Willoughby Hall's business?"

"We'd be delighted," Ben replied, beaming.

Mrs. Parker continued. "Since I'll be buying in quantity, perhaps we can negotiate on prices."

"Plus a discount for being a friend of the family," Josie added.

Ben pretended to be offended. "Hey, whose side are you on?" He grinned at Mrs. Parker. "I'm sure we can figure out something. Let me show you what we carry, and then we can sit down and make arrangements."

Cat was pulling on her coat. "Can I go? I want to call Marla." When Annie nodded, she yelled, "Nice seeing you, Mrs. Parker," and ran out of the door.

"Becka, why don't you take Michelle out and show her around," Annie suggested. "Josie and I can take care of customers while Ben's with Mrs. Parker."

Michelle looked up at Becka eagerly. "Sure," Becka said. "Come on, Michelle." She put on her coat and led Michelle outside. "That's our house across the street."

"It's beautiful," Michelle breathed.

Becka looked at it. Of course, in *her* opinion, it was beautiful because it was home. But objectively, she knew it was a run-down old farmhouse that needed a lot of work. "Want to see inside?"

Michelle's head bobbed happily. Her enthusiasm couldn't have been greater if she'd been invited to Disney World. And as Becka took her through the house, Michelle responded to each room with oohs and aahs.

When they entered the kitchen, Cat was just hanging up the phone. "Did Marla get picked to be a cheerleader?" Becka asked her.

"She won't find out till tomorrow morning," Cat replied. "What are you two doing?"

"I'm showing Michelle around."

38

"Better not take her into my room," Cat warned. "It's a disaster." She sailed out of the kitchen.

"What does she mean, 'a disaster'?" Michelle asked Becka.

"She means it looks the way it always does, like it's just been hit by a tornado. She hardly ever makes her bed and she leaves her clothes all over the place."

Michelle was shocked. "But doesn't she get into trouble for that?"

Becka shrugged. "Annie says if Cat wants to live like that, she can. It was awful when we were all sharing a room, because Josie and I aren't anywhere near as messy. We're all a lot happier now that we've got our own rooms."

If Michelle's eyes had been wide before, now they were saucers. "You each have your own room?"

Suddenly, Becka felt uncomfortable. Was she showing off, making Michelle even more aware of being an orphan? But Michelle was so eager for information. As Becka continued her tour of the house, she asked question after question. "When's your bedtime?" "Do you get an allowance?" "What happens if you get in trouble?" "Do you and your sisters ever fight?"

Becka answered patiently. She didn't mind,

really. They were the same things she'd wondered about when she was an orphan.

As they went into Becka's bedroom, Michelle noticed the ring on Becka's finger. "That's pretty."

Becka fingered the tiny ruby. "Our parents gave one to each of us when we were adopted. See, we met Annie and Ben in July, and the ruby is July's birthstone. Annie says this ring symbolizes our birth as a family."

To her horror, Michelle's eyes welled up with tears.

"Oh, Michelle, I'm sorry!" Becka grabbed a tissue from the box by her bed.

"That's okay," Michelle mumbled, wiping her eyes. "It's just that, well, this is like my dream. Having a family and a real home . . . "

Becka put her arms around the younger girl and hugged her. "I know. It was my dream, too."

"And your dream came true," Michelle said, hope springing into her eyes.

Becka smiled and nodded, but she was feeling more and more uneasy, like she was leading Michelle on. What had happened to her and Cat and Josie had been pretty unusual. Despite what Becka had told Michelle back at Willoughby Hall, the stories the orphans told were true. Older kids hardly ever got adopted.

Of course, Michelle was only nine, not that old. But most parents wanted babies. Which was too bad. It seemed to Becka that a sweet, polite girl like Michelle would make a perfect daughter.

Michelle was studying a framed photo of the Morgan family on Becka's dresser, and her face was taking on a wistful look again. Becka decided she'd better get her out of the house. "Let's take a walk."

It was cold outside, but the snow was gone. Becka took Michelle around to the back of the house, pointing out the garden and the barn.

"Wow, a real horse!"

"That's old Maybelline, our mare. Would you like to ride her?"

"Gee, I've always wanted to ride a horse. I've never been on one before."

"Maybe you'd better not, then," Becka said. "I wouldn't want you falling off and hurting yourself. Maybelline's very gentle, but – "

"*That* horse doesn't look gentle," Michelle said.

Becka looked in the direction she was pointing. "Oh, that's Red MacPherson on his horse, Belinda. Red lives next door." She waved to him, and Red steered his horse in their direction.

"Hi, Becka, what's up?"

"Hi, Red. This is Michelle. She's from Willoughby Hall, where Cat and Josie and I lived."

Michelle reached out and stroked the horse's nose.

"Hi, Michelle. Want to take a ride?" Red hopped off Belinda.

"She's never been on a horse before," Becka told him.

"I'll ride with her," Red said.

Michelle's eyes lit up and she looked at Becka. "Go ahead," Becka encouraged her.

Michelle giggled nervously. "Okay." Red hoisted her up so she could get her foot in the stirrup and pull herself onto the horse. Then he mounted up behind her.

Keeping one arm around Michelle's waist, Red guided the horse slowly. Becka walked along beside them.

"This is fun!" Michelle squealed.

They went all the way over to the Mac-Pherson property. Red's mother was outside, sweeping the path.

"Hi, Mum," Red called. Becka said hello, too, and introduced Michelle.

"Would you kids like to come in for some cocoa?" Mrs. MacPherson asked.

A few minutes later, they were sitting around the table in the MacPhersons' cozy kitchen. Becka and Red started talking about school.

42

After a while, Becka was afraid they were ignoring Michelle, but she realized that Mrs. MacPherson and the younger girl were talking happily.

"How about another cup?" Mrs. MacPherson offered.

It was a tempting offer, but Becka couldn't take her up on it. There was a knock on the back door, and it opened.

"*There* you are," Annie said. "Becka, I've been looking all over for you two! Mrs. Parker's ready to leave."

"Oh, I'm sorry," Becka said. "I forgot the time. I'll take her back to the store right now."

"Goodbye," Michelle said. "Thanks for the ride, Red. And thanks for the cocoa, Mrs. MacPherson."

"You're very welcome, dear. Come see us again."

Annie remained behind to chat with Mrs. MacPherson. Becka and Michelle left and headed back across the street. "I like them," Michelle said. "Is Red's father nice, too?"

"Red doesn't have a father. He died when Red was a baby."

"Oh." Michelle considered this. "Then I'll bet he half understands what it's like to be an orphan. Oh, Becka, this has been so much fun today!"

43

"Maybe you can come back for a real visit soon," Becka said.

"I'd like that." Before they walked into the store, Michelle turned and looked back at the house. "Becka, do you believe someday I'll have a real home and a family, like you?"

Becka looked down into her shining eyes. She couldn't bear to tell her that it wasn't likely. Maybe she should be more optimistic. After all, surely there was somebody in this world who would want this girl.

The words spilled out before she'd even formed them in her mind. "You'll have a home, Michelle. *I'll* find you a home."

Three

"Do you know anyone who wants a nine-year-old sister?" Becka asked Cat and Josie as they walked up the steps to school. Snow had started to fall, and they hurried into the lobby.

"Oh, sure," Josie replied. "Why, just the other day, I heard someone say, 'What I really want for my birthday is a nine-year-old sister.'"

"I'm serious," Becka said. "I have to find a family for Michelle."

"Why do *you* have to find a family for Michelle?" Cat asked.

"Because I promised her I would."

"Very smart, Becka," Josie said. "How do you plan to go about doing that? Take out an ad in the newspaper?"

Becka ignored Josie's sarcastic reference to the mistake she had made not long ago. "I don't know. But Michelle needs a home. We've got to help her."

"Why?" Cat asked. "No one helped us find a home."

Josie hooted. "There goes the noble, unselfish Cat." Then she looked directly at Becka. "Hey, what's this 'we' business? You told Michelle *you* would find her a family."

"But you guys will help me, won't you?" Becka pleaded. "Please?"

Josie groaned. Cat smiled, which gave Becka hope, until she realized the smile wasn't aimed at her. Turning, she saw Bailey, Cat's new boyfriend, coming in the door and towards them. He greeted them all cheerfully, brushing the flakes of snow off his jacket.

"Boy, I love this weather!" he announced.

"Must be a big change for you after living in California," Josie said. Bailey had moved to Green Falls only a month or so earlier.

"No kidding. Back there we had one season all year."

"Is this school different from the one you went to?" Becka asked.

"Oh, Becka," Cat said. "A school is a school. They're all alike." She tossed her hair and gave Bailey her famous sidelong glance. "Of course, maybe Bailey has a special reason for liking this school more than his old one . . ."

Bailey gave her a meaningful look. "Yeah, maybe I do."

"Oh, *please*," Josie muttered.

Bailey grinned at her. "You know, I started appreciating school when I had to be out for a week while my parents moved. Not going to classes," he added hastily. "Just being with people. It's lonely when you're an only child. You guys are lucky to have each other."

At that, Josie made her usual gagging sound, but Becka eyed him with interest. "Do you wish you had brothers or sisters?"

"Sure," Bailey said. "It might take some of my parents' attention off me."

Cat caught on to what Becka was getting at. "Becka, you're not about to ask what I think you're going to ask, are you?"

"Why not? Bailey, how would you like to have a nine-year-old sister?"

Bailey blinked. "Huh?"

"We know the sweetest girl who happens to be an orphan," Becka told him. "I know you'd love her."

"Becka!" Josie exclaimed. "You can't just walk up to people and ask them to adopt a kid!"

Bailey was taken aback. When he recovered, he smiled apologetically. "I'm sure she's terrific. But if my parents had wanted another child, they would have had one."

"But you could ask them, couldn't you?" Becka persisted.

"Becka!" Then Cat was distracted. "Look, there's Marla. I want to find out if she made the cheerleading squad."

"Wait," Becka said. "I don't think you need to ask." They watched Marla walk across the lobby. One look at her slumped shoulders and woebegone face told them the answer.

Cat put her lunch tray down at her regular table in the cafeteria. Britt and Trisha were eating at an unusually rapid rate. "Where's the fire?" Cat asked her lunchmates.

Trisha spoke with her mouth full. "We've got an assignment due next period that we both forgot about. We have to get to the library."

"Where's Marla?"

"She had to stop by her locker," Britt said.

"I can't believe she didn't make the cheerleading squad," Cat said, sitting down. "Who did, anyway?"

Trisha made a face. "Blair Chase."

Cat's mouth fell open. "Blair? That's impossible! She can barely walk in a straight line!"

"Yeah, but the cheerleaders were making the decision," Britt told her. "And they got a little pressure from their captain."

Cat should have known. Blair was Heather

Beaumont's best friend. Cat's eyes drifted over to the table where Heather was sitting with her usual group of admirers. Blair was one of them. "That's disgusting. Why do people always do what she tells them to? Nobody *really* likes her."

"I've been trying to figure that out since third grade," Trisha said. "I think she puts spells on people. Maybe she's a witch."

"I can think of a rhyming word that would describe her better," Britt said with a wicked glint in her eyes.

Cat laughed half-heartedly. "Guys, we have to think of some way to cheer Marla up."

Britt and Trisha agreed. "But how?" Trisha asked.

"Shh," Britt hissed. "Here she comes now."

Cat turned. "Hey, you know, she doesn't look like she needs cheering up." Marla's expression had changed dramatically since that morning. As she carried her tray to their table, she was greeting people with a bright smile.

"Maybe she's faking it," Britt said.

If so, it was a great performance. Marla was grinning from ear to ear and her eyes were sparkling as she joined them. "Wait till you guys hear this!"

"What happened?" Trisha asked.

Marla sat down. "Guess what I just found stuck on my locker door?"

Cat took a stab at it. "A note?"

Marla nodded.

"From who?" Britt asked eagerly. "Steve Garner?"

Marla wrinkled her nose and shook her head. "Better than Steve Garner."

"Well, that includes about ninety-five percent of the male student body," Cat said. "Come on, tell us. Which guy sent you a note?"

Marla grinned mischievously. She was obviously enjoying the suspense. "I didn't say it was a guy."

"Tell us!" Trisha demanded.

Marla laughed. "I'll let you read it. No, I'll read it to you." She extracted a plain white envelope from her purse and pulled out a sheet of paper. She paused dramatically, then began to read.

"'To Marla Eastman. From the Student Council.'"

Cat smiled, but the opening was a letdown. It must be another committee appointment. What was so thrilling about that?

Marla continued, reading slowly, savouring each and every word. "'It is our great pleasure to inform you that you have been selected as a nominee for Winter Carnival Princess.'"

There was a moment of utter silence. Then Britt let out a shriek, and Trisha clapped her hands. Marla happily accepted their congratulations.

"That's fantastic!" Cat exclaimed. It was great seeing Marla look excited and full of life again. But she had a question. "What's a Winter Carnival Princess?"

"It's part of the whole celebration," Britt explained. "There are three nominees, and the school votes on them. The Princess is crowned at the basketball game. It's supposed to be a secret, but it always leaks out before the game."

Cat beamed at Marla. "This should make up for all those bad things that have been happening."

Marla nodded. "Of course, I'm not the Princess yet. I have to be elected."

"You will be," Trisha said with conviction.

"I guess I have a decent chance," Marla said. "But I wonder who the other nominees are."

Cat's eyes roamed around the cafeteria to see if she could spot any other girls looking particularly excited.

"Gee, I hate to leave this celebration, but I have to go to the library," Britt said. "You do, too, Trisha."

"We'll try to find out who the other nominees are," Trisha said as she rose. "See you guys later."

"It doesn't even matter who they are," Cat

51

assured Marla. "You're going to win. I feel it in my bones. Besides, you're one of the most popular girls at school."

She realized Marla was looking past her at Heather Beaumont. "Yeah, but there are other popular girls. And some of them are awfully persuasive."

"You think Heather's one of the nominees?"

"I don't know." A look of uncertainty clouded Marla's face.

"Well, there's one way to find out." Cat rose from her seat. Luckily, Heather's table was right by the water fountain. Cat walked over, took a drink, then smiled brightly at the girls gathered around Heather.

"Congratulations," she said.

Heather's cold green eyes met hers. "Are you speaking to me?"

"Well, no, actually, I was congratulating Blair. I heard she's going to be a cheerleader. Is there some reason I should be congratulating you, too?"

Two of the girls started giggling. Heather smiled smugly. "Oh, you'll find out sooner or later." And then Cat spotted it – a plain white envelope, identical to Marla's, lying by Heather's tray.

Cat went back to her own table and reported what she had seen to Marla. She watched all the happiness evaporate from Marla's face.

"Oh, well," Marla sighed. "I guess it was nice being nominated."

"Cut that out," Cat said firmly. "Stop being so negative! That's not like you. Just because Heather was nominated doesn't mean she's going to win."

"She beat me when we ran against each other for pep club vice-president last year," Marla reminded her. "And she kept me from becoming a cheerleader."

"So what? The whole school is voting, remember? You've got more friends than Heather."

"Yeah, but for some reason Heather always gets her way."

"Not this time," Cat said with determination. "I always get my way, too, you know." She thought for a minute. "I'll get my sisters to help. Josie can pull in the basketball vote. Becka can work on the brains. And *I'll* get everyone else!"

A tiny smile began to form on Marla's face. "You think you've got that much influence?"

Cat didn't have to fake any modesty around Marla. "There isn't anything I've wanted badly enough that I haven't got if I've worked at it. And I've decided I want you to be Winter Carnival Princess."

She was pleased to see the effect her words had on Marla. She wore a real smile now, and a little of that old self-assurance had returned to her eyes. "Gee, Cat, I don't know what I'd do without you. You're a real friend. You're really going to help me get this?"

"I promise." Cat got up. "I have to run by my locker before class. I'll call you tonight and we'll start planning our strategy."

Annie was right, Cat thought as she left the cafeteria. It *did* give her a nice feeling inside, knowing she could help Marla get something she wanted so much. It was almost as nice as getting something for herself. Besides, Marla's grumpy mood was beginning to get on her nerves.

"Cat, wait up!" Becka appeared by her side. "This is so depressing. I've asked a dozen kids if they want a little sister. Nobody's showing the least bit of interest."

"That was a dumb promise you made to Michelle."

"Yeah, maybe, but I can't do anything about that now."

Personally, Cat thought Becka was being ridiculous, but she was in such a good mood she could afford to be kind. "You're going about this the wrong way," she advised. "Don't ask kids. They don't make those kinds of decisions. You need to be talking to grown-ups."

"I guess you're right," Becka said.

"And besides," Cat continued, "you can't expect people to want a kid they've never even seen."

Becka nodded. "Maybe I can ask Ben and Annie if she can visit us on Saturday. Then we could take her to the basketball game and show her around."

"There you go, saying 'we' again," Cat said. "This is *your* problem, not mine."

"Come on, Cat, you've got to help me," Becka wheedled. "I'll bet you're going to need *my* help one of these days."

Cat recalled the conversation she'd just had with Marla. "You know, for once in your life, you're right. There's something I do need your help with." She told Becka about Marla's nomination for Winter Carnival Princess. "I promised her we'd help get her elected."

"Fine," Becka said promptly. "You help me find a family for Michelle, and I'll help get votes for Marla."

"All right," Cat said. "It's a deal."

"Hey, there's something on your locker," Becka said.

Cat stood very still. Becka was right. Taped to her locker door was a familiar-looking plain white envelope. She stared at it in disbelief.

"Aren't you going to see what it is?" Becka asked.

Cat could feel her heartbeat speeding up as

she ripped the envelope off her locker. She opened it and pulled out a sheet of paper.

Becka read aloud over her shoulder. "'To Catherine Morgan. From the Student Council. It is our great pleasure to inform you that you have been selected as a nominee for Winter Carnival Princess.'"

Reading the words and hearing them at the same time still didn't make them real. Cat read the line over and over, checking to make sure that it was really her name on top. A tingle started in her toes and shot all the way up through her entire body. She could almost feel the Winter Carnival Princess crown on her head. She was dizzy, she was floating, she was riding on a cloud.

She turned to Becka in ecstasy. But Becka wasn't smiling. Her words brought Cat back down to earth with a thud.

"*Now* who's making dumb promises. Still want me to help get votes for Marla?"

Four

The benches in the gym were packed on Saturday afternoon. To Becka, it seemed like half the town had turned out to watch the Green Falls Junior High basketball team play Sweetwater. The action on the court had been non-stop, but Becka was more interested in the audience. For her purposes, the bigger the crowd, the better.

"I've never been to a real basketball game before," Michelle said. "This is so exciting!"

Becka could barely hear her over the noisy and enthusiastic fans. And responding was impossible, because just then a roar went up from the crowd.

Behind Becka, her father bellowed, "That's my girl!" Michelle was hopping up and down. "Wow, I can't believe Josie got that basket!"

Becka smiled, clapped her hands, and nodded, but she hadn't really been paying attention. She was too busy scanning the crowd for prospective parents for Michelle.

At the end of the first quarter, Mrs. MacPherson turned around. "Are you enjoying this, Michelle?"

"It's great! Josie's scoring more points than anyone!"

While they talked about the game, Becka studied a figure sitting a few rows below them. It was Mr. Davison, one of her teachers. Becka considered Mr. Davison's qualities. He was handsome, funny, and he handled their rambunctious class easily. She figured the woman by his side must be his wife. She wished she could get a good look at her face.

In the same row, Becka saw her friend Louise Nolan, with her parents. Louise was always telling Becka how lucky she was to have sisters. Louise only had one older brother, who was constantly teasing her.

"Josie got the rebound!" Michelle squealed.

"That's nice," Becka said vaguely. She was making a mental note of where Mr. Davison and Louise were sitting. Then she started to examine the occupants of the other benches.

"Becka, are you looking for somebody?"

Becka turned to Red, who was sitting on her other side. "Sort of." She glanced back at Michelle, who was completely engrossed in the game. Even so, she lowered her voice and spoke directly into Red's ear. "I'm looking for people who might want to adopt Michelle."

Red's eyebrows went up. Then Becka felt a hand on her shoulder. "Becka, watch," Annie said excitedly. "Josie's got a foul shot."

Becka wasn't even sure she knew what a foul shot was, but she directed her attention to the court. The audience became quiet, and all eyes were on Josie. She stood there, clutching the ball. For a moment, Becka forgot her mission and shivered, imagining how nervous Josie must be. Even though she couldn't really see Josie's face from where she was sitting, she could imagine the tense determination of her expression.

Josie aimed the ball and tossed it. The ball sailed up through the air and fell through the basket, barely ruffling the net. An ear-shattering cheer filled the gym. Relieved, Becka returned to studying faces.

Finally, the second quarter was over and the players left the court. In the stand, people stood up and stretched, or began milling around. Becka took Michelle's hand. "Come on, let's walk around."

"Where are we going?"

"I want you to meet some people." She gave Michelle a once-over, adjusted her hair clip, and examined her face. "Let's see a nice big smile."

Michelle obliged, baring her teeth. Becka thought about instructing her on charming behaviour, but she didn't want to make Michelle nervous. Clutching Michelle's hand tightly, Becka pushed through the crowd down to where Mr. Davison was sitting.

"Hello, Mr. Davison."

He smiled. "Hello, Becka." He turned to the woman next to him. "Honey, this is one of my students, Becka Morgan. Becka, this is my wife, June Davison."

Becka liked the way he called his wife "honey". That meant they had a good relationship. And she was pleased with Mrs. Davison. She was attractive, but not glamorous – sort of motherly looking.

Becka nudged Michelle forward. "This is Michelle. She's visiting us from Willoughby Hall. That's where I used to live, before I was adopted." For special emphasis, she added, "When I was an orphan. Like Michelle."

Unfortunately, the Davisons didn't catch that. Their attention was diverted to a small girl sitting in front of them, tugging at Mrs. Davison's sweater. "Mum, can I have another cookie?"

While Mrs. Davison reached for her purse, Becka spoke to her teacher. "Is that your daughter?"

"One of them," Mr. Davison replied. "I've got five in all."

Becka gulped. "Five daughters?"

He grinned. "And on a teacher's salary."

Becka smiled thinly and nodded. There was no point in pursuing this. "Nice seeing you, Mr. Davison. Come on, Michelle." She pulled her across the row, towards Louise. Then she spotted someone else – Mademoiselle Casalls, her French teacher, with her new husband. They were holding hands.

Becka greeted them and introduced Michelle. Mademoiselle Casalls responded with her usual cool elegance. "Bonjour, Becka, Michelle." Becka loved the way she said the name "Michelle". It dawned on her that Michelle must be a French name. That was a good sign.

Her husband spoke pleasantly to them, too. "Michelle's visiting us from Willoughby Hall," Becka began. But before she could use words like *orphan* or *adopted*, Mademoiselle's husband began whispering in her ear. Mademoiselle ducked her head and began giggling softly. It was like Becka and Michelle weren't even there.

Lovebirds, Becka thought. They seemed more like teenagers than possible parents. She could see there was no point in wasting time on them.

Still holding Michelle's hand, Becka led her over to Louise. "This is Michelle," she announced. "Michelle, this is my friend Louise Nolan and her parents."

"Hello, girls," Mrs. Nolan said in a friendly voice. "Are you visiting, Michelle?"

"I'm from Willoughby Hall," Michelle said. It was apparent that the Nolans knew what Willoughby Hall was. Becka was pleased to see the appropriate looks of sympathy on their faces.

"Your sister's playing a great game," Louise noted.

"Yeah, I'm real proud of her," Becka replied. "It's great having sisters."

She couldn't blame Louise for looking at her oddly. Becka was much more likely to complain about her sisters to Louise than praise them.

"Did you see Mr. Davison over there?" Louise asked.

Becka had an inspiration. "Yes. Did you know he has five kids?"

"Five!" Mrs. Nolan exclaimed. "My goodness. I wonder how they manage. I've got my hands full with two. If I had any more, I would just give up."

Becka's smile drooped. "Well, nice seeing you. Come on, Michelle."

"Congratulations, Cat!"

Cat glanced at the passing classmate. "Huh?"

"I heard you've been nominated for Winter Carnival Princess."

"Oh, yeah," Cat said. "Thanks."

After the classmate moved on, Bailey turned to her. "You're going to have to be friendlier than that if you want votes," he said in a teasing voice.

Cat nodded. He was right, of course. Normally in a situation like this, she wouldn't need reminding. She'd be out there talking to everyone, flirting with the boys, gushing compliments to the girls. If there was one thing she knew how to do well, it was how to be popular.

She tried to concentrate on the image of herself as Princess. But every time she conjured up a mental picture of herself with a crown on her head, another picture took its place. Marla.

She gave Bailey a bright smile. "Maybe I'd better go do a little campaigning. I'll be right back."

She went up a few rows, to where she'd seen Marla sitting with Britt and Trisha. But Britt and Trisha were alone.

"Where's Marla?"

"She's around somewhere," Britt said. Both of the girls looked at her uneasily, and Cat couldn't blame them. Ever since the day the nominations had come up, things had been strange. They all still sat together at lunch, but it wasn't the same. They talked about everything but the Winter Carnival. Marla avoided speaking directly to Cat. There were no more daily telephone conversations. When they ran into each other at school, they were polite. But each time they met, Cat could see the hurt in Marla's eyes.

"Here comes Marla now," Trisha said. Cat turned and saw her making her way up the stand. She paused at each row, to smile and chat. *Campaigning*, Cat thought.

When Marla saw Cat, her smile seemed to fade.

"Hi, Marla," Cat said. To her own ears, her words sounded falsely bright.

"Hello, Cat," Marla replied coolly.

"Great game, huh?" Trisha said loudly. "Looks like we just might beat Sweetwater this year."

"Yeah, great game," Britt echoed. "I think Josie's scored more points than any boy on the team."

Marla nodded. To Cat, she said, "You Morgan girls certainly know how to take over, don't you?"

Cat choked back a gasp. How could her best friend speak to her like that?

Luckily, there was a distraction.

"Don't look now, but guess who's coming

this way," Britt muttered. It was Heather, looking particularly cute in her little cheer-leading outfit.

Cat tried giving Marla that special look they always shared when Heather was around. If nothing else, surely they were still united in their dislike of her. But Marla wouldn't even meet her eyes.

"Hi, girls," Heather drawled. She focused her attention on Marla and Cat. "I don't think I've congratulated you two on being nominated for Winter Carnival Princess."

"Why, thank you, Heather," Cat said sweetly. "I'm sure you're just as happy about that as we are."

"Actually, I am." Heather tossed her head. "You two have the same friends. That means you'll split the vote." She laughed, as if it were a joke, but Cat knew it wasn't.

Having made her point, Heather moved on. Cat glared after her. "Honestly, she makes me so sick. One of these days, she's going to be sorry."

"Is that a promise or a threat?" Trisha asked.

"Both," Cat replied.

Marla spoke in a quiet, even tone. "And we all know how much a promise means to you."

"Uh, the game's starting again," Britt announced quickly.

Cat returned to her seat.

★   ★   ★

65

Josie could feel the perspiration dripping down the side of her face. She understood now why Green Falls hadn't won a game against Sweetwater in two years. Sweetwater was *good*.

Which wasn't to say Green Falls was playing badly. Every member of the team was doing his – and in Josie's case, her – very best. They followed the plays that Coach Meadows had made them practise, and it was a good policy. The coach obviously knew what Sweetwater could do, and all his instructions to the team had been designed around Sweetwater's strengths and weaknesses.

Unfortunately, Sweetwater didn't appear to have many weaknesses. What they did have were three players who were pretty tall for junior high students. And the tallest one could do a real dunk shot, something Josie had only seen in professional basketball on television.

Somehow, though, Green Falls managed to hold its own, and the score was very close. Over on the Sweetwater side, the boy dribbling the ball was surrounded by Green Falls players. Josie could see that the dribbler was trying to get into a position where he could throw the ball to that unbelievably tall guy on their team, so he could make another one of his amazing dunk shots.

But the Green Falls boys were doing their

best to prevent this. Every few seconds, one of them got the ball away, but a Sweetwater player kept getting it back.

Josie blocked out the noise of the crowd and the cheers of the cheerleaders, and put all her mental energy on Alex, who was closest to the dribbling Sweetwater boy. *Come on, Alex, get in there*, she ordered silently.

And then, Alex did. He was immediately surrounded by Sweetwater boys, and he was in no position to get the ball to Josie. He threw the ball to Gary Cole. Josie darted within Gary's range of vision and threw up her arms. She was in a good tossing position.

Gary had to have seen her. But he didn't throw the ball. He started dribbling. Josie realized in dismay that he was going to try for a basket. *What an idiot*, she fumed. There was no way he could get close enough to shoot, not with those Sweetwater guards already heading in his direction. Even if he did get close enough, Josie doubted that he could clear the net. If he couldn't do it in practice, what made him think he could do it now?

Josie moved faster than she ever had in her life. Luckily, no one was paying attention to her. She dashed forward and snatched the ball away from Gary. Her action took the Sweetwater players by surprise, and she

67

actually was able to get a few feet closer to the basket before taking careful aim.

The ball went through the net, and now the score was tied. With only a few seconds remaining, Sweetwater got the ball and started towards the other end of the court. But Todd swept in, grabbed the ball, and took a wild shot. It was in!

The crowd went wild. For the first time in two years, Green Falls had beaten Sweetwater. For a second, Josie just stood there, trying to catch her breath. Then she turned to her teammates.

They were gathered in a group, shrieking and cheering, slapping one another on the back, and giving one another high fives. Josie hurried over to join them. But just as she reached the group, they all took off, running towards the boys' locker room.

She paused a moment, watching after them, then started off in the opposite direction. Passing the stand, she saw Annie and Ben waving and making victory signs with their hands. Josie waved back. Several kids called out to her, yelling stuff like "Congratulations" and "Great game". That was nice. But she really wanted to be exchanging comments like that with her teammates.

It was lonely in the girls' locker room. Josie hurriedly showered and changed, not even bothering to dry her hair. Annie would have a fit if she knew Josie was going out in the cold with a wet head, but Josie didn't want to keep her teammates waiting. Surely they'd want to go out and celebrate their victory.

Emerging from the locker room, she saw the boys gathered at the end of the hall by the school exit. She walked towards them, pulling on her coat, and didn't see Gary Cole by her side till he spoke.

"Thanks a lot, Josie." They were words she'd expected to hear but definitely not spoken in that tone. There was no mistaking the resentment and sarcasm in his voice.

"What do you mean?"

"That was my big chance," Gary said. "You stole that ball right from under me."

"Gary, I just wanted us to win! Look, we're all in this together, right?"

"Oh, give me a break," he muttered. He ran over to the others, and in a loud voice, said, "Party's at my place, guys! Let's go!"

Josie just stood there and watched as the boys headed out of the door without her. A second later, she was surrounded by her parents, her sisters, and assorted friends. She could feel their hugs, hear their congratulations, Becka yelling, "Yay, Josie!"

But all she was really aware of was a great big lump in her throat.

Slowly, Becka replaced the telephone receiver. Then she scratched a name off her list.

Annie came into the kitchen, took the lid off the pot on the stove, and breathed deeply. "Mmm, Josie really has a talent with stew." She dipped a spoon in and tasted. "Becka, try this and see if you think it needs to simmer a little longer."

Becka obliged. The stew tasted perfect to her, but she wanted to make some more phone calls. "I think it should sit a few more minutes," she said.

"All right," Annie said, but she didn't leave the kitchen. "I'll put the noodles on to boil."

Becka looked down at her list. She still wanted to try Lisa Simon and Patty Jackson. Lisa was an only child, and Patty only had one brother, away at college. Either of them might like the idea of a kid sister.

"You've been on the phone quite a bit this evening," Annie noted. "Some big project going on?"

"I guess you could call it a project," Becka said. Annie glanced at her curiously, but she didn't ask any questions. She was always good about not prying into the girls' lives, waiting instead for them to come to her with problems. And they usually did. But Becka had an uneasy feeling Annie might not give her wholehearted

70

approval to Becka's promise to Michelle. More than once, Becka had been admonished for biting off more than she could chew.

"I'm sorry if I was tying up the phone," she said. "Did you want to make a call?"

"It's not urgent," Annie said. "I just want to thank Helen MacPherson for driving Michelle back to Willoughby Hall. I think Michelle enjoyed herself today, don't you?"

That was a good opening. "I wish I could find parents for Michelle," Becka began tentatively. "She really wants a family."

Annie nodded. "I wish there were homes for all the orphans in the world. And Michelle is such a darling child."

Those were encouraging words. Becka was just about to blurt out what she was up to when the phone rang. She picked it up. "Hello?"

"Uh, could I speak to Cat, please?"

The voice was familiar. "Just a minute." She covered the mouthpiece and yelled, "Cat!"

A second later, Cat appeared. "Is it Marla?" she whispered.

Becka shook her head. "It's a boy." She wasn't surprised to see Cat's face fall slightly. But Annie's eyebrows went up, and now her curious look was directed at Cat.

Cat took the phone. "Hello? Oh, hi, Todd."

Annie busied herself pouring noodles into the boiling water, but Becka didn't bother to disguise her interest. It had been a long time since Todd had called.

"No, I'm busy tonight," Cat said. There was a pause. "No, I can't get out of it. I don't *want* to get out of it. Goodbye, Todd." She hung up.

"*Honestly*," she mumbled.

"I thought you said you weren't going out tonight," Annie said.

"I'm not," Cat replied. "Bailey has to do something with his parents. But I still don't want to go out with Todd. I don't know why he called. He knows about Bailey and me."

"Can't blame a guy for trying," Annie said lightly. "Todd's a nice boy, Cat."

"You think I should have gone out with him?" Cat asked. She cocked her head thoughtfully. "I guess it wouldn't hurt to make Bailey feel like he's got some competition."

"Oh, no, Cat," Annie said. "I'm not suggesting you go out with Todd. Not if you don't have any feelings for him. That would just be using him."

Cat looked at her blankly, and Becka suppressed a giggle. Cat had never had a problem with using people to get what she wanted.

Just as they were all sitting down to dinner, the phone rang again. Cat jumped up from her seat. "I'll get it!" A moment later she was back. "That was Mrs. MacPherson," she told Annie. "She said not to disturb you, just call her back after dinner." She kept looking back at the kitchen, as if she was waiting for the phone to ring again.

"Expecting an important call?" Ben asked as he served the stew.

Cat shrugged. "I just thought that might have been Marla."

"Have you guys had a fight or something?" Josie asked.

Cat gave her an aggravated look. "Josie, you *know* we were both nominated for Winter Carnival Princess."

"Oh, *that*." Josie made it clear how totally unimportant that was to her.

Annie looked more sympathetic. "Is that causing a strain on your friendship?"

Cat nodded. "See, I promised Marla I'd help her win the election. But that was before I knew *I* was going to be nominated, too."

"Making promises like that can be dangerous," Ben said.

"I know that *now*," Cat said.

Annie reached over and patted her hand. "I'm sure that once the election's over and done with, you and Marla can go right back to being friends again."

"I don't know," Cat said. "She really wants

to be Princess. She's going to hate me when, I mean if, I win."

"Well, at least you've learned something," Ben said, smiling. "Be careful before you make promises you might not be able to keep. Becka, don't you like the stew?"

Becka looked down at her barely touched plate. "Oh, I like it," she said quickly, and started eating. But Ben's words were ringing in her ears. *Be careful before you make promises . . .*

"The stew's delicious," Annie said. "I was just thinking that we might make this for Tuesday night."

"What's happening on Tuesday night?" Ben asked.

"Don't you remember? We've invited the Laytons for dinner," Annie told him.

Becka's head jerked up.

"We could ask Helen MacPherson, too," Annie said. "Do you girls want to invite anyone? Cat, what about Marla?"

Cat brightened. "Yeah, that's a great idea."

"Josie, how about you?" Ben asked. "One of the kids from the basketball team?"

Josie shook her head. "No, I don't think any of them would be interested."

"Oh, come on," Ben urged. "I'll bet any one of those boys would like to have dinner with the team star!"

74

Becka spoke up. "Can I invite Michelle?"

"Of course," Annie said. "But it's a school night. I'm not sure she'd be able to get permission from Mrs. Scanlon."

"Maybe you could call Mrs. Scanlon and ask her," Becka said. "She wouldn't say no to you. And it would mean so much to Michelle. She loves being here. *Please?*"

Annie seemed a little puzzled by the urgency in Becka's voice, but she nodded. "All right, I'll call tomorrow."

Satisfied, Becka began eating her stew with gusto. The Laytons! She hadn't even considered them. They were good friends of her parents, and they'd just moved to Vermont a few months ago to open an inn. They didn't have any children, and they were always saying how much they admired Annie and Ben's decision to adopt. Why hadn't she thought of them sooner? They were the absolutely perfect parents for Michelle!

Five

On Tuesday afternoon, Cat strode briskly down the hall and stopped at the open door to the *Green Gazette* office. She looked in at the students milling around inside, but she didn't see Becka. Folding her arms, she tapped her foot impatiently.

"Hi, Cat," a skinny boy with glasses greeted her.

"Hi, Jason. I was looking for Becka."

The newspaper editor nodded. "I just saw her. She's on her way. I guess you must be getting excited about the election for Winter Carnival Princess on Friday."

Cat hesitated. Now was the perfect time to turn on the charm full force. After all, Jason was a pretty influential person. Oh, if only this were just a battle between herself and Heather. And if only she could erase the image of Marla's disappointed face from her head.

She compromised and offered a modest smile. "Oh, sure. Jason, could you give Becka a message for me? Oh wait, never mind." She spotted Becka coming towards the room.

"Tell Annie and Ben I'm going to Brownies with some friends, okay?" Cat asked her.

"I can't," Becka said. She cocked her head towards the *Green Gazette* office. "I've got a newspaper meeting."

"Darn," Cat muttered. "I guess I'd better call them."

"Don't forget, we've got company coming for dinner," Becka reminded her. "Cat, what do you think of the Laytons? Don't you think they'd be perfect parents for Michelle?"

"How should I know?" Then Cat saw Josie heading towards her locker. "Hey, Josie! Tell Annie and Ben I went to Brownies, okay?"

Josie gave a nod to indicate she'd heard and kept on moving.

"Come on, Cat," Becka pressed. "You promised you'd help me find parents for Michelle."

"Yeah, but that was only because you promised to help Marla be Winter Carnival Princess. And you're off the hook on that one. So I don't have to keep my promise to you, either."

Becka put her hands on her hips. "Are

you saying sometimes promises count and sometimes they don't?"

"I'm saying – I'm saying . . . " Cat stopped and rubbed her head. She didn't know what she was saying. It was all getting too complicated. If she heard one more word about promises, she was going to scream.

"Excuse me."

Cat turned. It was the last person in the world she wanted to see. "What do you want, Heather?" she asked testily.

"I'd like to get into this room, but you're blocking the door."

"This is the *Green Gazette* meeting," Becka said.

"I know what it is," Heather replied. "I'm interested in joining the staff." With that, she breezed by them into the room.

Cat watched her, incredulous. "Heather Beaumont on the newspaper staff? That's crazy! It's not even one of the cool activities."

Becka disregarded the insult. "I don't think that's why she's really here. I bet she just wants to hang around and get votes for Winter Carnival Princess. She was at the French club meeting this morning, and she's not even taking French! And Louise Nolan told me she showed up at the science club meeting yesterday, acting like she wanted to join."

That was enough evidence to convince Cat

that Becka's suspicions were correct. Only brains and geeks belonged to the science club. "What a sneaky scheme," Cat said.

"Yeah," Becka agreed. "I'm surprised you didn't think of it first."

"Mmm," Cat murmured. "Of course, then Marla would really hate me. See ya later."

But how much more could Marla hate her? Cat pondered as she went off to join her friends. Marla was still shooting Cat odd looks and barely speaking to her. She'd turned down Cat's invitation to dinner that evening without even making up a good excuse.

Britt and Trisha were waiting for her by the school exit. "What took you so long?" Britt asked.

Cat told them about seeing Heather in the newspaper meeting. "She's just faking an interest to kiss up to those kids. You know how she can turn on the charm when she wants to. The kids who don't really know her always fall for it. Ooh, she gets me so mad."

"You always find ways to get back at her," Trisha offered as comfort.

"But what can I do?" Cat complained. "I can't start really campaigning to win, or Marla will *never* speak to me again. Everything's bad enough as it is."

"I asked Marla to come to Brownies with

us," Britt said. "She said she'd meet us there if she finished some work she has to do in the library."

Cat brightened. "That's good. Oh, I hope she comes."

"Well, I didn't tell her you were coming, too."

"Oh." Cat stamped her foot in frustration. "What's the matter with her, anyway? I didn't *ask* to be nominated!"

"She just keeps saying you promised to help her win," Britt said.

"It'll all be over soon," Trisha said. "The election for Winter Carnival Princess is on Friday. And I've got a connection with a guy on the Student Council. He's going to let me know the results as soon as the votes are counted."

"Personally, I don't care who wins," Britt said. "As long as it's not Heather."

"Right," Trisha agreed. "I'll be happy if either you or Marla wins."

"Oh, sure," Cat said. "That's how I feel, too." She hoped her words rang true. She wasn't convinced that they were. Winning would make Marla awfully happy. But in the back of her mind, she could hear the words *Princess Cat*. They had such a nice sound.

★ ★ ★

80

Josie fumbled around in her locker for her books. Thank goodness there was no basketball practice that day. She was in no mood for Gary Cole's dirty looks.

Todd Murphy approached her. "Josie, do you know where Cat is?"

"She went to Brownies."

"Okay." He started to walk away.

"Todd, wait. I want to talk to you about the team."

"What about it?"

She ignored the look of discomfort on his face. "Do you think I'm any good?"

He shrugged. "Yeah, sure."

"Do the other guys think I'm good?"

He shifted his weight from one foot to the other, making it clear that he wanted to escape this inquisition. But Josie wanted some answers. "Do the guys think I'm a good basketball player?"

"Well, yeah, I guess so. Hey, you scored more than half the points in the last game."

"Then why do you guys act different around me than you act with each other?"

He struggled to find the right words. "Because, you know, it's like, well . . . " Finally he blurted it out. "You're a girl!"

Josie clutched her head. "What's that got to do with anything?"

Todd looked at her as if she were un-believably stupid. "The guys aren't used to having a girl in the team. Boys act different around girls than they act around other boys."

"Then stop thinking of me as a girl," Josie demanded. "Consider me just another team member."

Todd's eyes swept over her jeans and unruly short hair. He actually seemed to be considering the possibility. Then he shook his head. "Nah. Wouldn't work."

"But this is ridiculous!" Josie exclaimed. "They should appreciate me! I'm one of the best players in the team!"

"Yeah, you're right," Todd admitted. "But I guess that's the problem."

"Huh? What does *that* mean?"

"Well, you score a lot of points. The coach is always telling you how good you are. And he's always yelling at the rest of us. Maybe some of the guys don't like that he never finds anything wrong with you."

"Some of the guys," Josie repeated. "You mean, like Gary Cole?"

Todd nodded. "Yeah. You can't blame him, really. The way you play, it makes him look bad."

"But practically every guy on the team is better than he is," Josie protested. "Why doesn't he hate them?"

82

"I guess he doesn't care if the guys are better. But you're a – "

"I know," Josie interrupted. "I'm a girl." She slammed her locker door shut with unusual force. "Well, thanks for the information, Todd."

"No problem," Todd said, and he took off.

Josie leaned against her locker and sighed. Her thoughts went back to the conversation she'd had at Willoughby Hall with Mrs. Parker. What had she said? *Play the best game you can, and the boys will love you?* Hah! It seemed to her that the opposite was true.

It's hopeless, Josie thought dismally as she walked towards the exit. As long as she was a girl playing a good game, the boys would never accept her.

Then she stopped. Okay, there was nothing she could do about being a girl. But maybe there was something she could do about her game.

There was the usual after-school crowd in Brownies. Britt, Trisha, and Cat slid into a booth and tried unsuccessfully to flag down a harried-looking waitress.

Karen Hall and Sharon Cohen stopped by their table. Karen spoke to Cat. "We've been trying to decide who to vote for on Friday, you or Marla."

"And we finally came up with a solution," Sharon chirped.

"Tell us," Britt demanded.

Karen beamed proudly. "One of us will vote for Cat and one of us will vote for Marla!" With that, the two sailed away.

Britt turned to Trisha. "I guess that's what we'll have to do, too."

"Great," Cat said glumly. "You see what's happening? It's just like Heather said. Marla and I will split the votes of the people who like us. So Heather's going to win."

"There's only one way Heather can lose," Trisha said. "If we get all the kids we know to vote for Marla. Or for you," she added hastily. "What do you think?"

Cat didn't know what to say. She was almost glad to see Todd approaching their table. At least he'd save her from replying.

"Uh, Cat, could I talk to you for a minute?"

"It's a free country," Cat replied.

"Alone?"

Britt and Trisha were watching with interest. Making a show of reluctance, Cat rose. "All right." She followed him to a booth at the back.

"Okay, we're alone," she said. "Now, what do you want?"

84

Todd reddened. First he scratched his head. Then he coughed. Then he drummed his fingers on the table.

"See, the thing is, well . . . Cat, I've been thinking."

That's a change, Cat thought. But aloud, she asked, "Thinking about what?"

"About us. Maybe we shouldn't have broken up. We had some good times, remember?"

"I'll tell you what I remember," Cat responded coldly. "I remember that you dumped me and went running back to Heather Beaumount."

"Well, you were grounded," Todd said. "I had to go out with somebody."

Cat didn't know whether to laugh at him or yell at him. What Todd was basically saying was that he needed a girlfriend, and any pretty girl would do. It wasn't very flattering.

"Anyway, Heather and I are through," Todd continued. "So I think you and I should get back together."

Cat almost felt sorry for him. How could he be so dense? She tried to be kind. "Now, Todd, you know that Bailey and I – "

Todd interrupted. "Come on, Cat, it would be great. We could go to all the Winter Carnival activities together. You'll be the Princess and – "

Now it was Cat's turn to break in. "What makes you think I'm going to be the Princess?"

"Well, if we were going together, all the guys on the basketball team would vote for you. Football team, too. With those votes, you're bound to win."

Cat was so startled she was momentarily speechless. When she found her voice, she sputtered, "Todd! Are you trying to bribe me?"

Todd looked at her blankly. "Huh?"

With scepticism, Cat examined his face. But Todd's expression was totally innocent. She had to admit that Todd just wasn't smart enough to come up with a scheme that devious. He was just putting two and two together. If the guys knew that Cat was his girlfriend, he figured she'd be elected Winter Carnival Princess. Knowing how popular Todd was with his teammates, Cat had a feeling he was probably right.

Her head was spinning. She knew exactly what she *should* say. "No, thank you, Todd. You're a nice boy, but I've got another boyfriend now. We weren't all that good together anyway. Let's just be friends."

But the words wouldn't come. All five senses were going in her head and they blocked her power of speech. She could almost hear those words – *Princess Cat*. She could feel the crown being placed on her head, hear the cheers, see her photograph in the newspaper. Up to now, it seemed like a remote possibility. But Todd could help make it all happen.

"Well?" Todd asked impatiently. "How about it?"

"I – I don't know," Cat managed to say. "I have to think about it."

Todd groaned. "Jeez, Cat . . ." But just that minute, a bunch of guys walked into Brownies and spotted him.

"Todd! Over here!"

Todd got up. "See ya later," he told Cat.

She nodded and watched as he joined his friends. Then she glanced back at her own table.

Marla was there now, with Britt and Trisha. But Cat didn't go back to them. Luckily, Brownies was so crowded by now she could probably slip out unnoticed.

She could still feel that crown on her head. And she was afraid Marla might be able to see it.

Upstairs in her bedroom, Becka tied a ribbon around Michelle's hair. "There are some nice people coming to dinner tonight," she told the younger girl. "George and Sally Layton. They own an inn right here in Green Falls."

"Are the MacPhersons coming?" Michelle asked.

"Why, do you have a crush on Red?" Becka teased. "No, I don't think he'll be here, but his mother will. Now, when you meet Mrs. Layton, tell her about that A you got on your book report. And tell Mr. Layton how you climbed the ropes all the way to the top in gym."

"Why?" Michelle asked.

Becka hesitated. Should she tell Michelle she had to impress them, that the Laytons were a real possibility for parents? No, she decided, it was better not to get the orphan's hopes up, just in case things didn't work out. *But it has to work out,* Becka thought anxiously.

Michelle was still waiting for an answer. "Why should I tell them about my essay and climbing the ropes?"

"Oh, just to make conversation," Becka said. "They're nice people, so . . . so you want to be nice to them."

Michelle looked up at her solemnly. "I try to be nice to everyone."

Becka hugged her. "Of course you do. Just be especially nice to the Laytons, okay?"

Michelle still looked puzzled. Maybe she'd forgotten Becka's promise to her. But Becka hadn't. "Come on, let's go."

Downstairs, Becka checked out the living

room. Mr. Layton and Ben were sitting on the sofa, and Josie was sprawled on the floor in front of them. A peal of laughter from the kitchen told her Mrs. Layton was in there with Annie. She could see Cat in the dining room, putting candles on the table.

"There's Mr. Layton," she whispered to Michelle. "Doesn't he look like a nice man?"

Michelle followed Becka to the sofa. "This is Michelle Jones," Becka said. "Michelle, this is Mr. Layton."

"How do you do?" Michelle said, and put out her right hand to shake his. *She looks adorable*, Becka thought. *And definitely adoptable.*

Mr. Layton gave her a jovial grin and took her hand. "I'm very pleased to meet you, Michelle."

"Michelle was just telling me about a spelling test her class had at school," Becka said. "How did you do in that spelling test, Michelle?"

She pretended not to see the puzzled look Ben gave her. Michelle had already told them all about the spelling test when she arrived.

Michelle looked at her in confusion. "I told you before. I won."

"Isn't that terrific?" Becka asked, beaming. "Michelle's an excellent student."

"Congratulations," Mr. Layton said. "You must be quite a speller."

"Well, the words were pretty easy," Michelle replied.

"And she's so modest!" Becka continued. "Not at all conceited."

Michelle squirmed slightly, but Becka wasn't finished. "You're good in all your subjects, aren't you, Michelle?"

"Becka, you're embarrassing her," Josie stated.

"George, did you catch the Celtics game last weekend?" Ben asked.

"Yeah! Wasn't it a great one? That's what I call serious basketball."

"We took Michelle to see Josie play last Saturday," Becka said. "Michelle absolutely *loves* basketball. Don't you, Michelle?"

"I guess. That was the first game I've ever seen."

"But you like sports, right?" She mouthed the word *ropes* at Michelle.

"Becka or Josie!" Annie's voice rang out. "Could one of you come in here?"

"We'll go," Becka said to Josie. Grabbing Michelle's hand, she led her back to the kitchen.

"Hi, Mrs. Layton." She propelled Michelle forward. "This is Michelle."

"Hi, Michelle," Mrs. Layton said.

"Becka, would you put these napkins on the table?" Annie asked.

"I can do it," Michelle said. She took the stack of napkins from the table.

"Isn't she super," Becka gushed. "Offering to help like that! She's so cooperative!"

"She's a very sweet child," Annie murmured. Becka smiled at her gratefully and turned back to Mrs. Layton.

"Michelle lives at Willoughby Hall. Where Cat and Josie and I used to live. Before we were adopted."

"I still can't get over you and Ben having three daughters," Mrs. Layton said to Annie. "And it's worked out so well!"

Annie nodded. "We're very happy. But you wouldn't believe the reaction of some people when we told them we were adopting three!"

"I can just imagine," Mrs. Layton said with a laugh. "Adopting three children at once must be pretty unusual."

"But it's not so unusual to adopt just one," Becka said quickly. "Lots of people do it."

"Let's go into the living room," Annie suggested. "Becka, would you bring in that tray of cider, please?"

Passing through the dining room with the tray, Becka pulled Michelle away from where she was talking to Cat. "Come with me."

"Cat might be a princess!" Michelle said.

"I know, I know. Let's talk to Mrs. Layton."

But just as they entered the living room, Ben opened the front door to another guest.

"Mrs. MacPherson!" Michelle exclaimed, and hurried over to greet the Morgan's neighbour.

Becka frowned. It looked like she was going to have to continue to sing Michelle's praises for her. Michelle wasn't catching on to what she needed to be doing. Becka went around the room offering cider and finally got back to Mrs. Layton.

"Mmm, this cider is delicious," Mrs. Layton said.

"Josie made it," Annie told her. "And she taught me how to make the stew we're having tonight."

"You're lucky to have such a talented daughter," Mrs. Layton said with a smile.

Annie put an arm around Becka. "They're all pretty special. I don't know how we'd manage in the store without them."

"I'll bet you wish you had kids who could help you at the inn," Becka said.

Mrs. Layton misunderstood. "Why, thank you, Becka, but we've got a full staff now." She wisely didn't look at Cat when she said it, though Cat blushed anyway. A few weeks before, Cat had worked part-time at the inn – and it had been a disaster.

"I'm going to check on dinner," Annie

said, returning to the kitchen. Becka looked for Michelle. She was still in the midst of an animated conversation with Mrs. MacPherson.

"Did I tell you that Michelle is an orphan?" Becka asked Mrs. Layton.

"Yes, you did mention that. It's nice of you to take such an interest in her."

"She's very special," Becka said. "Don't you think so?"

"Well, I don't really know her," Mrs. Layton replied. "You should bring her over to the inn sometime for tea."

"When?" Becka asked eagerly.

"Oh, anytime you like." Her response was too vague to satisfy Becka.

Annie reappeared. "Dinner's ready, folks." As everyone headed towards the dining room, Becka began to feel desperate. Once they were all at the table, there would be lots of conversation and it would be harder to point out Michelle's virtues to the Laytons. This called for drastic measures.

"Mrs. Layton," Becka said urgently. "Wouldn't you like to have a child?"

Becka could have sworn Mrs. Layton's face became a little pink, and she smiled oddly. Becka understood the reason when they all gathered around the table.

"Sally and I have an announcement to make," Mr. Layton said. He put an arm around his wife. "We're going to have a baby."

Becka managed to keep a fixed smile on her face as a chorus of congratulations rose from the table. But a sickening disappointment filled her. She couldn't bring herself even to look at Michelle.

Six

The shriek from Coach Meadows's whistle pierced the gym. "Okay, that's enough. Over here."

The players gathered on the steps below Coach Meadows for the traditional after-practice assessment of their performance. Expectant faces searched his for some indication of his opinion, but Josie knew from experience there was no point in this. His expression never revealed what he thought of them. They had to wait for him to speak.

As the coach studied his notes, Josie pulled off her sweaty headband. As far as she could tell, this practice session had been pretty decent, but Coach Meadows had keener eyes than she had.

Finally, the coach spoke. "Johnson, you went out of bounds twice. Hayes, your dribble's getting sloppy. A baby could have taken that ball away from you." He continued making individual criticisms as his eyes surveyed the group. Eventually, he got to Josie. "Nice shooting."

Josie winced. Funny, in the past his praise had made her glow inside. Now, it only served to set her apart from the others. She could understand now what Todd had been talking about the day before. And if she needed any more confirmation of how the boys felt, Gary's hostile glance at her provided it.

Having completed his evaluation, Coach Meadows went on. "Now, about the game tomorrow. We all know Henderson Junior High is having a crummy season. Every school in the state has rolled over them. They've become the laughingstock of junior high basketball." He spoke in a quiet, even tone, his penetrating eyes moving from player to player.

"No one's expecting much of a match tomorrow. The fact that the game's at three-thirty on a weekday doesn't help. There won't be a big turn-out in the stands like there was last Saturday." He paused, and added with a hint of a smile, "We'll be lucky if the cheerleaders show up."

The group tittered.

"But don't get cocky!" Coach Meadows roared. The sudden change in tone made

Josie jump, even though she was used to this tactic. "A team can be a breeze one day and a hurricane the next. Henderson wants to win. Any team that wants to win can turn their record around overnight. So don't think you can play sloppy ball and still beat Henderson. You get out there tomorrow and play like you did on Saturday! Okay, hit the showers."

The boys leapt up and ran as a group to their locker room entrance. Alone, Josie went in the opposite direction to hers. But she didn't take her shower immediately. Instead she plunked her elbows down on the counter under the mirror and rested her chin in the palms of her hands.

Her thoughts went back to her first days at Green Falls Junior High. She recalled her disappointment at discovering there was no girls' basketball team, and her determination to get on the boys' team. She remembered how thrilled she had been when the boys agreed with the coach to let her join.

Now, here she was, a fully-fledged member of the basketball team. But she didn't *feel* like a fully-fledged member. No matter how well she played, the boys didn't consider her one of them.

Looking into her reflection, Josie realized something was missing. She clapped a hand to her forehead. Her headband – she'd left it on the court. She shuffled back out to the gym to retrieve it.

She thought the room would be empty, but it wasn't. Gary Cole was on the court, alone, shooting baskets. Or at least, trying to. Over and over he tossed the ball, and it went in every direction but into the basket.

Finally, he got one in. "Good shot!" Josie called.

It took less than a split second for the look of surprise on Gary's face to be replaced with a hostile look. "What's that supposed to mean?"

"Just what I said," Josie replied. "That was a good shot."

Now Gary's expression was a combination of hostility and suspicion. "I suppose you could do better."

Josie had no doubt of that, but she denied it. "I've just been lucky. I think we had a good practice today, don't you?"

Gary sneered. "Good for you, maybe. At least, according to Coach Meadows."

It was a major effort to keep smiling, but Josie was determined not to let him get to her. "I think he just tries to be nice to me because I'm new to the team. Hey, what do you think of that new play we worked on? The one where Todd fakes a throw, gets the ball to Alex, and he sends it to me?"

"I think it's another chance for you to show off," Gary replied shortly.

"If you don't like the plays, why don't you tell him?" Josie asked.

Gary snorted. "He doesn't listen to me."

"You want me to ask him?" It was the wrong question. Gary glared at her.

"Why? You think you've got more influence with the coach than I do?" He uttered a harsh laugh. "Yeah, you probably do. You're Coach's little pet. He doesn't even know what I can do because he never gives me a chance. If it wasn't for you . . . " His voice trailed off.

Josie was pretty sure the coach knew very well how little Gary could do. But as Gary began to stalk off the court, she called out, "Wait!"

Frowning, Gary paused. "What do you want?"

"Why did you say if it wasn't for me? What do I have to do with anything?"

"If it wasn't for you, maybe I'd have a bigger part in that play. Like, Alex could be sending that ball to me instead of you. Then I'd get the credit for the basket."

What basket? Josie wondered. If Gary had the ball, there was no way they could score.

99

Gary couldn't shoot from that distance. Her expression must have reflected her thoughts, because Gary turned away.

"Wait!" Josie called again.

Now Gary looked positively annoyed. He paused, but he didn't turn completely around.

What she was about to suggest was crazy, totally insane. But if she could win Gary over, the other guys would follow. It was worth the risk.

"Maybe . . . maybe you could take my part in that play."

He turned to face her. *"What?"*

"Like you said: Alex could send the ball to you instead of me."

Gary stared at her in disbelief. "The coach would never go for it. Once he sets a play, that's it."

Josie gulped. "Well, we wouldn't tell him. We'd just do it. We don't even have to tell Alex. Just stay close to me, and once I've got the ball I'll pass it to you."

Gary was speechless for a few seconds. "You – you're going to pass it to me?"

"Yeah."

He cocked his head to one side and eyed her thoughtfully, as if he was seeing her for the first time. "Really?"

"I promise."

Gary nodded. "Okay." And he took off.

Josie went over to the benches and picked up her headband. She clutched it tightly. What had she just promised?

It'll be okay, she assured herself. Like Coach Meadows said, Henderson had a weak team. Green Falls could afford to lose a couple of points.

It was worth it, to win some friends.

Sitting in a booth at Luigi's, Cat drummed her fingers on the tabletop and ignored the soda sitting in front of her. She glanced up at the clock on the wall. *Basketball practice should be over by now,* she thought. *Todd will be here any minute.*

That was assuming he got the note she had left on his locker. But it was a pretty safe bet. He always went by his locker before he left school.

Her eyes swept the restaurant. Thank goodness no one she knew was there. She wouldn't want this meeting to get back to Bailey. Of course, maybe it wouldn't hurt to let Bailey think he had a little competition. On the other hand . . .

She rubbed her head, wanting to erase thoughts of Bailey. His image dissolved, but it was immediately replaced by Marla's.

Hurry up, Todd, she thought. Cat didn't want to be alone with her thoughts. She wanted to stop remembering. But the memories kept flooding back.

Cat had met Marla here, at Luigi's, just a few weeks after she, Josie, and Becka had come to live with the Morgans. From the very beginning, she and Marla had hit it off. They had the same interests, they liked the same clothes, and they both hated Heather Beaumont. That last similarity had sealed their friendship. Throughout all of Cat's conflicts with Heather, Marla had been on Cat's side, giving her support, helping her battle Heather's nasty little schemes, and aiding her with her retaliations.

Marla had introduced Cat to all the right people at Green Falls Junior High. She had steered Cat in the right direction when it came to clubs and activities. They'd shared clothes, makeup, and lots of secrets.

Cat had never had a best friend before. Already, she missed Marla so much.

Cat took a sip of her soda and swallowed hard, trying to get rid of the lump in her throat. Why should she be feeling guilty? It was all Marla's fault, anyway. She shouldn't have tried to hold Cat to that stupid promise. There was no way Cat could keep it, not after being nominated herself.

So Cat might as well go all out and try to win.

She saw Todd coming in the door. How her heartbeat used to quicken when she saw him back in the early days of their romance! Now she felt absolutely nothing. But she knew how to act like she did.

"Hi," she said as he slid into the booth. Cat automatically cocked her head and gave him her sidelong look. The grin he returned assured her that she hadn't lost her touch with him.

"Hiya, babe."

Cat tried not to shudder. She hated to be called "babe." Bailey never called her that. "Were you surprised to get my note?"

"Not really," he said. "I had a feeling you'd come around." He looked satisfied, very pleased with himself. It was incredibly annoying.

"How was your basketball practice?"

That set him off on one of his long, dreary descriptions. Back when they went out together, during football season, Cat had learned to block out these descriptions mentally and use the time to plan her wardrobe for the next week. This time, she tried to pay attention but it was hopeless. Basketball was even more boring than football.

When he paused for breath, she broke in. "Think you'll have a good game tomorrow?"

"Oh yeah, we'll slaughter them," he replied.

"That's nice."

"You want to go out after the game?"

Cat was prepared for this. She lowered her eyelids, then raised them to reveal a look of sincere regret. "I can't, Todd. It's a school night. Annie and Ben have laid down the law about going out on school nights."

"But it doesn't have to be at night," Todd argued. "The game should be over by five-thirty. We could just go for a soda."

Cat had an excuse all ready for that, too. "I have to work in the store after school tomorrow. I won't even be able to come to the game."

Todd's forehead furrowed. "You were always able to get out of working at the store before."

"Well, Annie and Ben have become stricter. You know, making rules, giving advice . . ." It wasn't a total lie. Annie and Ben did give advice, when they were asked for it. In fact, she could remember a bit of advice Annie had offered recently, right after a call from Todd. *Don't go out with him if you don't care about him. That would be using him.*

Well, she wasn't actually planning to go out with him, just to let him think she would. Any date she made, she'd break – after the election.

At least Todd was buying her excuses. "I

But one of these days, Michelle would remember Becka's promise. She'd want to know where her family was. Becka would have to admit she'd failed her and witness the little girl's heartbreak.

These awful thoughts were making sleep impossible. *Maybe a rummage in the refrigerator will help,* Becka thought. She got out of bed and tiptoed out into the hall.

There was a light coming out from under Josie's door. Becka rapped lightly and went in.

Josie was sitting up in bed, her arms wrapped around her knees. She gave Becka a half-hearted smile. "Can't you sleep either?"

"No," Becka said. "It must be something in the air." She sat down on the edge of Josie's bed. "I just can't stop thinking."

"About what?" Josie asked.

"Keeping promises."

"Yeah." Josie grimaced. "It's really stupid, isn't it? Promising something without thinking about it first. And then you get stuck."

Becka agreed. "I shouldn't give up. But I can't think of anyone."

"What are you talking about?"

"A family for Michelle, of course. Isn't that what you're talking about?"

Josie shook her head. "I'm talking about *my* promise."

The door to her room opened again. Cat

107

was standing there. "What are you guys doing up?"

"We could ask you the same question," Josie replied.

"We can't sleep," Becka told Cat. "I guess you can't either."

"I could sleep if I wanted to," Cat said. "I'm just not tired." She plunked herself down on Josie's bed. "What's going on?"

"We were talking about promises," Becka said. "Josie made a promise she can't keep."

Cat groaned. "I don't want to hear that word." But she didn't leave.

Josie corrected Becka. "I didn't say I *can't* keep it. I'm just not sure I want to."

"What kind of promise?" Becka asked. She listened with interest as Josie told her about Gary Cole.

"Why did you tell him you'd pass the ball to him if he can't get it through the basket?" she asked.

"So the others would accept me," Josie explained. "So they'd treat me like one of the guys."

Cat wrinkled her nose. "Who wants to be treated like one of the guys?"

"*I* do," Josie replied. "But I shouldn't have to do something stupid like this. When you're on a team, you're supposed to do whatever you can do to help your team win. If I give this ball to Gary like I promised . . . well, we probably won't lose. But it certainly won't help us win."

"Then don't do it," Cat said.

"And break my promise to Gary?"

Cat shrugged. "Sure."

Becka was shocked. "Cat! Breaking promises is wrong!"

"You broke your promise to Michelle," Cat pointed out.

"But not on purpose!" Becka exclaimed. "At least I've tried to keep it. And I still might find a family for her."

"Oh yeah?" Cat challenged her. "Like who?"

Becka sat very still. An idea, something she'd never considered before, had suddenly sprung up in the back of her mind. Was it crazy? Totally unrealistic? Maybe not.

She spoke slowly. "How would you guys feel about having a little sister?"

Josie's mouth dropped open. "Becka!"

"Are you nuts?" Cat asked.

"Just listen," Becka said eagerly. "You both like Michelle. Annie and Ben do, too. They've got three daughters. What difference would one more make?"

This was probably the first time she'd ever seen Josie and Cat wearing the same expression – total, utter disbelief.

"It's not so crazy," Becka insisted. "Just think about it for a minute. Can you come up with one good reason why we shouldn't adopt Michelle?"

"*I* can," Cat said. "We've each finally got our own bedroom. And there aren't any more in this house."

"I'd share mine with her," Becka said. But even as she spoke, a little uncertainty crept into her voice. She loved having her own room.

"There's no point in even discussing this," Josie stated firmly. "It's not our decision to make. You have to ask Annie and Ben. But don't get your hopes up. Adopting three daughters was a pretty outrageous thing for them to do. No matter how much they like Michelle, I don't think they're up for a fourth."

Becka knew there was logic in what she said. "But it's the only way I can keep my promise to her!"

"Oh, Becka," Cat said in disgust. "You're making such a big deal out of this."

"Promises *are* a big deal," Becka shot back. "Maybe not to you, but – "

"Yeah," Josie interrupted. "I don't get it, Cat. Isn't Marla your best friend?"

Cat stiffened. "She was."

"I guess being Winter Carnival Princess must mean an awful lot to you," Becka said.

110

Cat was quiet for a minute. "Of course it does. Getting something like that . . . well, it means you're special."

Becka considered that. "I guess it's pretty exciting. But you'd only be special for one night."

Josie agreed. "I'll bet nobody even remembers who last year's Winter Carnival Princess was."

"The Princess gets her picture in the newspaper," Cat pointed out.

"And you know what people do with newspapers after they read them?" Josie asked. "Throw 'em in the garbage."

Becka spoke up quickly. "Or recycle them, if they care about the environment."

Josie shrugged. "Either way, they're gone."

"That's true," Becka said. "Being Winter Carnival Princess is a one-night deal. Friendships last forever." She could have gone on talking about the meaning of friendship, but the look on Cat's face stopped her. In fact, she was completely taken aback by the expression. Cat was as close to tears as Becka had ever seen her.

But when Cat spoke, her voice was harsh. "Okay, I made Marla a promise. But then I was nominated. There's nothing I can do about it now."

"Maybe there is . . ." Josie said slowly.

"What are you saying?" Cat's eyes darkened. Then she clapped a hand to her mouth. "You're not suggesting I withdraw my name from the candidates, are you?"

The horror in her voice made Becka feel really, truly sorry for Cat. But Josie was making a good point. "It's a way to keep your promise. Like I'm going to keep mine. And Josie . . . " She paused and turned to her.

"Yeah," Josie said in a tired voice. "I'll keep mine."

Becka turned back to Cat. "What are you going to do?"

Cat tossed her head, but the gesture didn't have the confidence it normally did. She rose from the bed and went to the door. "I'm going to sleep."

Seven

Becka was waiting for the right moment.

Breakfast in the Morgan household tended to be a cozy time. Annie always insisted that everyone needed a good, unrushed breakfast to get them all going. She made sure that they were all at the table on time and together, and she wouldn't tolerate any dawdling, not even from Cat. She didn't allow Ben to read his newspaper at the table, either. Breakfast was a family time, and it was usually a noisy time, with all of them talking about their plans for the day.

But not this morning. Silence reigned at the table. Josie ate her porridge methodically, like a robot who wasn't even aware of what was being eaten. Cat stirred hers listlessly with one hand, using the other hand to twist a lock of hair, a sure sign that she was preoccupied with her thoughts.

Becka was eating, but without giving much attention to her breakfast. She was too busy examining her parents' faces, trying to assess their moods. Her eyes darted back and forth between them.

"Mmm, this porridge is delicious," Ben remarked. "What did you put in it?"

"Cinnamon," Annie told him. "And nutmeg. It's a trick Josie taught me."

"It certainly doesn't taste like the bland porridge I used to get when I was a kid," Ben said. "Josie, did you learn this at Willoughby Hall?"

Josie blinked. "Huh?"

"Did Mrs. Parker at Willoughby Hall teach you to make this porridge?"

"Yeah."

Becka didn't miss the puzzled looks Ben and Annie exchanged. This might not be the perfect time, but at least Ben's words had given her an opening.

"Speaking of Willoughby Hall, don't you think Michelle is sweet?"

"Of course, dear," Annie said. But her attention was now on Cat. "Cat, you haven't touched your porridge."

"What?"

"Don't you like the porridge?"

Cat looked down at the bowl as if she was seeing it for the first time. "Oh yeah, it's terrific." But her tone was flat.

Annie glanced at Ben, and then bit her lip. Becka knew what that meant. She was dying to ask the girls what was bothering them, but she didn't want to pry.

She finally gave in. "Is there something you girls want to talk about? Or ask us?"

Ben picked up on that. "You know there's nothing you should ever be afraid of saying to us."

The right time had come. "Yes, there's something I want to ask," Becka announced. "It's about Michelle."

"What about her?" Ben asked.

Becka chose her words carefully. "Well, it's like this. We were talking last night, Cat and Josie and I . . . " She faltered. Her eyes beseeched Cat and Josie for help, but they were both lost in their own thoughts.

"Yes?" Annie said encouragingly.

"We were talking about Michelle." The next words came out in a rush. "She's so sweet and we really like her and we wondered if you and Ben might want to adopt her."

Their immediate reaction didn't surprise her. In her private fantasies, she'd imagined gasps of joy, applause, cries of "Why didn't we think of that first?". But in reality, she suspected the response would be pretty much what she was now seeing. Total astonishment.

Ben spoke as if he wasn't sure he had heard correctly. "Adopt Michelle?"

"She wants a family so much," Becka said. "She loves being with us, and she's comfortable here."

"Oh, Becka," Annie sighed. "Oh, dear." *That* wasn't very encouraging.

"Don't you like Michelle?" Becka asked.

"Of course we like her," Ben said. "She's a very nice little girl."

"I'm sure we'd like every orphan at Willoughby Hall if we knew them," Annie added. "And I'm sure every one of them would like a home. But honey, that doesn't mean we can adopt them all."

"We don't have to adopt them all," Becka said. "Just Michelle."

Annie gave her a sad, apologetic smile. "I'm sorry, Becka. But we just can't adopt another child. We're happy we've got you three – "

"But three daughters are about all I can handle," Ben teased. Then he caught himself. "I shouldn't joke. This must mean a lot to you."

"I knew you liked Michelle," Annie said. "But I didn't realize you'd become that attached to her. Cat, what about you?"

"Huh?"

"Do you feel that strongly about Michelle?"

"Michelle who?"

116

"Cat!" Becka exclaimed.

"Oh yeah, sure," Cat said hastily.

The slightest hint of doubt crossed Annie's face. "Josie? Did you want us to adopt Michelle?"

"It would have been okay with me," Josie said. But her voice definitely lacked any real conviction.

Annie and Ben exchanged looks.

"Becka, tell the truth," Ben said. "Why do you want us to adopt Michelle?"

Becka squirmed. Both her parents were waiting for an answer. She'd never been able to sweet-talk them like Cat. It was confession time. She gave them a weak smile. "Well, I sort of promised her I'd find her a family. And I can't think of anyone else."

Ben looked like he was about to explode. "Becka! You've got no business making promises like that!"

"Darling, we know you meant well," Annie added hastily. "But you can't make promises you're not capable of keeping!"

Becka hung her head. "I know that. *Now*."

Ben groaned. "I thought I had made myself perfectly clear on that subject before." He glanced at Cat. Now she began to squirm.

"But what am I going to say to Michelle?" Becka asked plaintively.

"Tell her the truth," Annie said. "Tell her

117

you wish you could help her, but you made a mistake in promising her a family, and that you're sorry."

"I just feel so awful about this," Becka moaned.

Ben reached over and stroked her head. "Well, we all make mistakes. Just chalk it up to experience." He turned to Josie. "At least you can learn from your sisters' mistakes and avoid getting yourself into a predicament like this."

Josie squirmed.

Well, it certainly didn't look like Becka was going to be able to keep her promise, Cat thought as she walked into school. She still didn't know about her own.

It was fairly quiet in the building. Becka had had to get to school early for a newspaper meeting, and if they wanted a ride, the other two had to come along, or else walk almost a mile through the slush of melting snow.

Cat ran into Bailey in the entrance hall. A smile spread across his face when he spotted her. "Hi," she said. "What are you doing here so early?"

"I have to use the library before school starts. But I wanted to see you first."

Fear closed her throat. Despite his smile,

she wondered if he'd found out about her meeting with Todd yesterday. "Why?"

"Just wanted to see you. No particular reason." His smile broadened. "I like looking at you."

Cat smiled back. He was really so sweet.

"Especially when you smile," he added. After a second, he asked, "What's wrong?

Cat was looking beyond him. "Check that out."

Bailey turned. Heather was at the other end of the lobby, surrounded by a bunch of boys. What made that unusual was the fact that they were all seventh-graders, and Heather never spoke to seventh-graders.

"They must be members of some club," Cat murmured. The boys were gazing at Heather in awe. They were obviously thrilled to have this pretty, popular eighth-grade girl paying attention to them. And they'd remember her name when it was time to vote for Winter Carnival Princess tomorrow.

Bailey read her mind and shook his head ruefully. "She's just using those poor guys. After tomorrow she won't even know them." He looked at Cat seriously. "I'm glad you're not like that, out campaigning for this thing. I mean, it would be nice if you win, but it's no big deal, really – why are you looking at me like that?"

119

She could have said something cute and flip and flirty. But she didn't. All she could do was repeat what he'd said to her. "Because I like looking at you."

He grinned. "I wish we could spend all day looking at each other, but I'd better get to the library. See you later."

She nodded and didn't try to make him linger. She had somewhere to go, too.

She'd already written out the note. It lay neatly folded between the covers of one of her books. She'd even remembered to put some tape in her purse so she could stick the note to the locker door.

But as she rounded the corner to the hallway, she saw that the note wouldn't be necessary. Todd was standing there, twirling the combination on his locker.

"You're here early," she said.

"Yeah, I've got detention for being late yesterday. Look, are you sure you can't get out of working at the store? We're going to mutilate Henderson this afternoon, and I'm going to feel like celebrating."

"No, I can't go out with you this afternoon," Cat said. She took a deep breath. "Or this weekend. Or ever."

Todd scratched his head. "What do you mean?"

"I mean . . . I mean, I've had some time

120

to think it over. And I don't want to get back together with you."

He still looked puzzled. "Why not?"

She recited the words on her note from memory. "Because I don't care about you, not that way. You're a nice person and I hope we can be friends, but that's all." She marvelled at how adult she sounded.

Maybe too adult for Todd. Confusion remained on his face. "I don't get it."

Cat sighed. She reached into her book and pulled out the note. "Here. Read it over a few times. It's got to sink in eventually."

She turned away and went back down the hall. The first part of her mission was accomplished. Now came the hardest part.

The main office was empty. Cat waited a minute, then called, "Hello?"

Ms. Sanders, the secretary, emerged from the principal's office. "Hello, Catherine. What can I do for you?"

Cat took a deep breath. "It's about the election for Winter Carnival Princess."

Ms. Sanders looked at her reprovingly. "The election's tomorrow, Catherine. And you know the results are kept confidential until Winter Carnival week."

That's what you think, Cat thought. From what she'd heard, the entire student body knew who won within hours of the vote. But aloud, she said, "Oh, I'm not interested in the results, Ms. Sanders. It's about the ballot."

Ms. Sanders pursed her lips. "The names are listed alphabetically, Catherine. Your name cannot come first on the ballot."

Cat was getting annoyed. It was bad enough having to do what she was about to do, without Ms. Sanders misinterpreting her intentions. "I don't *want* my name to come first. In fact, what I want you to do is . . . is . . . " Why was she having such a hard time saying it? Maybe because it was such an out-of-character thing for her to be doing.

It took every ounce of willpower she had to finally get the words out. "I want you to take my name off the ballot."

Ms. Sanders looked dumbfounded. *"What?"*

Cat held her head high. "I wish to withdraw my candidacy."

The secretary's eyebrows rose. "You don't want to be the Winter Carnival Princess?"

Odd, how some lies came easily to her while others were caught in her throat. "No . . . "

"I find that difficult to believe," Ms. Sanders stated.

Cat forced herself to look directly into the secretary's eyes. They were bright with interest. Cat felt a sudden, urgent need to confide. This mature, impartial, down-to-earth woman might be just the right person.

Plus, Cat wanted to prove to Ms. Sanders that she really wasn't the kind of girl the secretary seemed to think she was – someone who was just out for herself. Or maybe she just wanted to prove that to herself.

She leaned across the desk and said softly: "See, Marla Eastman is one of the candidates, and she's my best friend. I want her to win."

The secretary's lips twitched. "And you think she can't win if *you* are on the ballot?"

Why did this woman have to make her sound like she was so conceited? But she didn't want to go into the whole complicated story, so she just nodded.

"Marla Eastman is a very popular and well-liked student," Ms. Sanders said. "I believe she has as good a chance as you have to be selected."

"I just want to help her – " Cat began, but the secretary wouldn't let her finish.

"It's too late anyway," the woman said briskly. "The ballots are already prepared."

Slowly, Cat let out her breath. She just stood there deflated for a minute. Then she murmured, "Thanks anyway," and left the office.

Becka and Josie were waiting outside. "I saw you go in there," Becka said, her eyes wide. "You really did it! You took your name off the ballot!"

"I never thought you had it in you," Josie said with grudging respect.

Cat didn't even allow herself a moment to bask in their admiration. "I tried, but it was too late. The ballots are already made."

"Oh." Becka's shoulders slumped. "Then I guess you won't be keeping your promise either."

"Boy, we *are* a bunch of idiots," Josie mumbled.

Cat wasn't about to lump her serious situation in the same category as their silly promises. "Speak for yourself." She started to walk away, but then she stopped and turned back. "Hey, Josie, when you have your game this afternoon . . . "

"What about it?"

Cat drew herself up proudly. "Tell the guys to vote for Marla."

As if the guys would listen to her, Josie thought, remembering Cat's request. Well, she had to give Cat some credit. At least she was making a stab at keeping her promise. Sometime in the next few minutes, Josie would have to make a decision about hers.

So far, Coach Meadows had been right about this game. There weren't many people in the stands, just some classmates who didn't have anything better to do after school. The few cheers she heard were pretty weak. Even the cheerleaders didn't seem to be leaping as high as they normally did.

She could understand why every school in the state had rolled over Henderson. These guys were pathetic. They were into the fourth quarter, and the score was fifty to twelve. Green Falls could afford to do without her points today, Josie thought. It would be easy to pass a ball to Gary. If the coach questioned her about her action later, she could always say she got confused, or she forgot the play, or something.

Josie was suddenly aware of the ball coming in her direction. She made a dash for it, but it was too late, and one of the Henderson guards caught it.

It was so hard to keep her mind on the game! Over and over, she saw herself sending that ball to Gary, which amounted to sending it directly to the opposition. Okay, Coach Meadows wouldn't like it, but only she'd know she'd done it on purpose. Well, Gary would know, but he'd never tell. Everyone would forget about it. Except her. She would know that she'd deliberately done something that was not in the best interests of the team. It would be sitting on her conscience.

"Morgan!" someone yelled.

Josie realized a Henderson player was about

to go past her, dribbling the ball. She darted forward, and easily slipped the ball away from him. Dribbling, she headed down towards their basket. Then she caught Gary's eye.

Would this be a good time to send the ball to him? She could get it over with. But as she was debating, some pipsqueak from Henderson moved in front of her. Suddenly her ball was gone.

There were only a few minutes remaining. Josie began to hope that maybe she wouldn't have to make a decision about Gary. The play where she'd promised to pass the ball to Gary couldn't go into effect unless Todd got the ball from Alex. And Todd hadn't been playing as well as usual. He seemed to be having a hard time concentrating, too. He might miss the ball completely. If the play never went into motion, it would cancel her promise.

But her hopes were dashed when a Henderson forward, in a feeble attempt to throw the ball to one of his teammates, sent it almost directly into Alex's hands. Alex moved as if he was about to throw the ball to the player on his left, then quickly turned and tossed it to Todd.

Todd woke up. He pretended to aim toward the hoop. Then he threw the ball towards Josie.

Josie grabbed it. Frantically, her eyes searched the court for Gary. But he was so far away! Why hadn't he come closer to her, like she'd told him to? Even if by some miracle he could catch her ball, there was no way, absolutely no way he could get it in the basket.

There were only seconds left. Everyone's eyes were on her. Gary was waiting for her to keep her promise.

But Josie couldn't. It was wrong. She'd made a very stupid promise. Just like Becka and Cat, she couldn't keep it.

She threw the ball at the hoop. For what seemed like an eternity, the ball teetered on the rim of the basket. Then it fell off the side.

Of course, it didn't really matter. They'd still win. At least she'd blown the points honestly.

Josie couldn't even hear the buzzer that signalled the end of the game. She was thinking about facing Gary.

But first, she had to face Coach Meadows. They all did. And despite their win, the coach did not look happy.

"You guys were lucky!" he thundered. "You sure didn't win that game with skill! I've never seen such sloppy playing in my life! Murphy, you were a space cadet! Benson, I don't think you moved twelve inches out there!" He whirled around. "Morgan! You weren't even watching the ball! You didn't even aim for that last basket!"

"I'm sorry," Josie mumbled, but the coach had gone on to reprimand someone else.

"You make me sick, all of you!" he yelled. "If you don't shape up, I'm going to be looking for a new team!" With that and a final look of disgust, he marched out of the gym.

No one seemed very upset by his comments. They were all used to the way Coach Meadows yelled and criticized and threatened.

"Hey, we weren't *that* bad," Todd said.

"Yeah, Henderson wasn't worth too much effort anyway," another boy commented.

"Look, we won, didn't we?" Alex slapped a player on the back. Now that the coach was out of sight, they all went into their usual post-victory performance – back slapping, high fives, rustling each other's hair.

So far, Josie had managed to avoid Gary. But any minute now he'd confront her. She started to slink away.

Then she felt it. A slap. On her back. She turned in disbelief. Gary stood there. "So Miss Perfect wasn't so hot today, huh?" He was grinning.

There was another slap on her back. She wasn't even sure who it came from. Alex ruffled her hair. It dawned on her that there were other guys around her. She wasn't on the outside of the circle.

"Come on, let's go to Luigi's," one guy yelled. There was a general chorus of agreement. For the first time, Josie knew the invitation included her.

Eight

"Was that the phone?" Cat asked anxiously, pulling herself up to a sitting position.

"No, honey, it's the tea kettle," Annie replied. She rose from the rocking chair and went back to the kitchen. Cat let out a deep, heart-wrenching sigh and lay back down on the couch. It was already seven o'clock on Friday evening. How long did it take to count ballots, anyway?

Ben was moving logs in the fireplace with a poker, sending the flames higher. "For a city fellow, I think I've become pretty darn good at this. Isn't this a beautiful fire, girls?"

"Beautiful," Cat muttered.

"Yeah, it's beautiful," Becka echoed, in the same dismal tone.

"Boy, you guys are a couple of deadbeats," Josie announced. "Ben, this has got to be the most gorgeous fire in the state of Vermont. Maybe in the universe."

"Thank you, Josie," Ben said.

Annie returned with her tea and sat down by Cat. "Ah, this is nice. A quiet, cozy family evening at home, just us."

Ben agreed. "But it would be even nicer if we could see happy faces on all our daughters."

Josie faced her sisters with her hands on her hips. "Cheer up, you guys. Look, we all tried. We did our best. Like you said, Ben, we all make mistakes, right?"

"Right," he replied. "Though I must say, Josie, I'm still amazed that all three of you got yourselves into these predicaments."

"Oh well, that's life," Josie said. "It's all over and done with. We can't mope forever."

"That's easy for you to say," Becka murmured. "You didn't keep your promise, but everything worked out for you."

"Yeah, weird, isn't it," Josie responded cheerfully.

"Do you think Gary forgot about your promise?" Annie asked.

"No," Josie said. "He told me he couldn't get close enough for me to throw it to him. But he thinks I would have thrown it to him if he'd been in the right position. As long as he thinks that, he'll believe I kept my promise! Personally, even though he'd never admit it, I think Gary stayed away from me on purpose. He must know what a bad player he is."

"Then why did he agree to go along with you in the first place?" Becka asked.

"He just wanted to see if I *would* do it. It was like a test. He thought I always wanted to show off and be the team star. I'm sure he was really happy when I didn't make that last basket."

Ben stopped poking at the fire and eyed her quizzically. "Did you miss that basket on purpose?"

"No," Josie said. "I was just having a bad game. It happens." She gave them a cocky grin. "Even to me."

"It all worked out for the best," Annie said.

Josie nodded happily. "Now that the coach has yelled at me like he yells at them, they can accept me."

"I don't understand," Becka said. "You play badly, and the guys like you better. It doesn't make sense."

"Sure it does," Josie argued. "Look, I've been playing really well so far this season. The guys were jealous."

"Boys can be so immature," Cat said.

"Exactly," Josie said. "But as soon as I messed up, they saw that I'm not perfect." She snapped her fingers. "Poof! Now I'm one of them."

Listening to Josie chatter was making Cat feel even more disgruntled. There was something very annoying about Josie's happiness, when she herself was so tense and irritable. She looked at Josie through narrowed eyes. "I don't suppose you remembered to do what I asked you to."

Josie went blank. "What did you ask me to do?"

"Tell your teammates to vote for Marla."

"Oh. No, I forgot."

"Figures," Cat grumbled.

"When do you find out who won?" Annie asked Cat.

"We're not supposed to find out until the Princess is announced at the Winter Carnival. But Trisha has a connection on the Student Council who's going to call her tonight as soon as they've counted the votes. Then she's going to call me."

"Who did you vote for?" Josie asked Becka.

"Don't ask her that," Ben admonished. "This is America. Voting is a private matter."

"For crying out loud," Josie said. "We're not exactly talking about President of the United States."

Cat stirred restlessly. The phone hadn't rung in ages. "Do you think the phone might be out of order?"

A shrill ring provided an immediate answer

to her question. Cat leaped up. "I'll get it."
She flew out of the room.

"Hello?"

"Hello, Cat, this is Helen MacPherson. Is
your mother there?"

Cat heaved another sigh. "Just a minute,
I'll get her."

She went back to the living room. "Annie,
it's Mrs. MacPherson." Annie got up and left
the room. Cat flung herself back down on
the sofa.

"I wonder if I should call her," Becka
mumbled.

"Call who?" Josie asked.

"Michelle."

"Oh, quit worrying about her," Cat ordered.
"I'll bet she's forgotten all about your
promise."

"Sure she has," Becka retorted. "Just like
Marla's forgotten yours."

Annie returned. "Helen and Red are going
to drop by in a bit. She says they have a surprise
for us."

She'd barely finished speaking when there
was a knock on the door. "Good grief, that
was fast," Ben said.

But it wasn't Helen MacPherson. Cat jerked
up at the sound of the familiar voice.

"Hello, Mrs. Morgan. Is Cat home?"

"Yes, Marla, come in."

Cat rose from the couch, turned, and faced her. "Hi, Marla."

"Hi, Cat."

For a few seconds, they both just stood there, their eyes not really meeting. From the floor, Becka and Josie stared at Marla with undisguised curiosity.

"Um, I wanted to talk to you," Marla finally said. The word *alone* was unspoken, but Cat knew Marla well enough to hear it.

"Come on up to my room."

Marla followed Cat up the stairs. Once they were in Cat's room, Cat sat down on her bed, while Marla kept standing. "Why don't you take your coat off?"

"I can't stay long."

"Oh."

There was a moment of silence. Then, as casually as she could, Cat asked, "Have you heard from Trisha yet?"

Marla shook her head. "Have you?"

"No."

Marla went over to Cat's dresser and began to examine her perfume bottles. "It's going to be weird for someone, finding out she's going to be Princess. And then having to pretend she's surprised when it's officially announced."

"Yeah," Cat replied.

135

There was another moment of silence. "I came to tell you I'm sorry," Marla said.

"Sorry?"

Marla smiled sheepishly. "I've been a real jerk. I should have known you'd keep your promise."

Cat looked at her in total confusion. Dimly, she heard a phone ringing downstairs. A second later, she heard Josie's voice bellow, "Cat! It's for you!"

Cat went to the door. "I'll get it up here," she yelled back. She went into her parents' bedroom and picked up the receiver.

"Hello?"

"Cat, it's Trisha."

Cat listened very carefully as Trisha relayed her message. Then she went back to her room.

"What were you saying about my promise?"

"I didn't find out till this afternoon. One of the guys on the basketball team told me."

"Told you what?"

"Oh, come on, Cat, you know what you did."

Cat looked at her uncertainly. "Tell me what you heard."

"I heard that Todd Murphy told all his buddies to vote for me."

For a moment, Cat didn't comprehend what she was saying. "Todd did what?"

Marla rolled her eyes. "Quit acting like you

don't know anything about it. It's common knowledge that he still has a major passion for you. I know you must have gotten him to do it."

Suddenly, it all made sense. It must have finally penetrated Todd's thick skull that Cat wasn't going to start seeing him again. He got angry, and wanted to get back at her. He certainly wouldn't tell the guys to vote for Heather, after she'd dumped him. The only way he could ensure that Cat wouldn't win was to make the guys vote for Marla."

"I know it couldn't have been easy for you," Marla continued. "Playing up to him when you don't really care about him anymore. But you did it for me." Her eyes were shining. "Oh, Cat, I've been so awful. You really are a friend."

Now that she'd recovered from her confusion, Cat could smile modestly. "Well, after all, I did promise to help you."

"And you kept your promise. That's what really matters. Win or lose, I don't really care anymore." She unbuttoned her coat. "Maybe I will stay a while. Who was that on the phone? Bailey?"

"No, it was Trisha."

Marla looked almost comical, frozen with her coat dangling off one arm. "What – what did you say?"

Cat fingered a lock of hair. Should she enjoy the drama of the moment for a while? No, that would be too cruel. For days, she'd felt like she was wearing a crown on her head. Magically, it had turned into a halo.

She cocked her head and eyed Marla thoughtfully.

"How good are you at acting surprised?"

Becka couldn't believe her ears when she heard peals of laughter coming from upstairs. A moment later, Cat and Marla came running down.

"May I have everyone's attention?" Cat asked. "I'd like to present to you the next Green Falls Junior High Winter Carnival Princess!"

Becka gasped. While Annie, Ben, and Josie congratulated Marla, she examined Cat's face. She didn't even look upset.

"I owe it all to Cat," Marla told them. "I know she must have wanted to be Princess, but she sacrificed that for me. She promised me she'd help, and she did!"

Josie gaped. Ben and Annie were staring at Cat as if they were trying to figure out who had taken over their daughter's body. Becka was incredulous. "She did? How?"

Cat shot her a fierce look. Then she smiled at Marla. "Let's keep that to ourselves."

Ben and Annie still wore identical expressions of disbelief. But they didn't press the question.

Annie got up. "This calls for a celebration. Josie, want to give me a hand in the kitchen?"

Ben went to the stereo and put some music on. Cat started quizzing Marla on what she would wear for the crowning and who she would ask to be her escort. A few moments later, Annie and Josie reappeared with a cake and a pitcher of cider.

Becka curled up closer to the fire and observed the celebration through dull eyes. It wasn't fair. She and Cat and Josie had all made the same stupid mistake. But she was the only one who was still suffering.

When the doorbell rang, she didn't stir, even though she was the closest to the door.

"That must be the MacPhersons," Annie said.

She was right. The door opened to Helen and Red MacPherson. But they weren't alone.

Becka stood up. "Michelle!"

The little orphan ran across the room and threw her arms around Becka. "Oh, Becka," she said. "Thank you!"

"For what?" Becka asked stupidly.

"What's going on?" Annie asked in bewilderment.

"I wanted you all to meet someone very

special," Helen said, her warm eyes resting on Michelle.

"We already know Michelle," Josie said.

"You know Michelle *Jones*," Mrs. Mac-Pherson corrected her. "This is Michelle MacPherson. Or at least, she *will* be. As soon as the final adoption papers are signed."

Annie squealed and clapped her hands while Ben embraced Mrs. MacPherson. Josie let out a whoop. Red swooped Michelle up in the air.

Becka was in a state of shock. When the full impact of Mrs. MacPherson's announcement finally hit her, she felt almost dizzy. Then Mrs. MacPherson came over and embraced her. "We owe this to you, Becka. Why, if you hadn't brought Michelle to visit, we might never have met."

"I didn't even know you were considering adoption," Annie said.

"Neither did my mother," Red said laughing. "But every time she saw Michelle, she'd go on and on talking about her. And when I reminded her that I'd always wanted a kid sister – "

"That clinched it," Mrs. MacPherson finished.

Michelle was hopping up and down. "I'm going to have a mother and a brother and my own room and a horse – golly, Becka, when you promised you'd find me a family, I didn't really believe you could. But you did it!"

"I did it," Becka repeated in wonderment. "I don't know how. But I did it!"

Bailey arrived a few minutes later. Then a couple of guys from Josie's basketball team dropped by. The quiet family evening turned into a real party.

The MacPhersons were the last to leave. A sleepy-eyed Michelle clung to Red's hand as Becka accepted more thanks from Mrs. MacPherson.

"This is amazing," Josie remarked when the family was finally alone. "None of us could really keep our promises. But everyone *thinks* we did. And everything worked out the way we wanted it to!"

Ben looked sceptical. "It seems to me that you're all taking a lot of credit for things you haven't really done."

"Actually, in a way, I *did* keep my promise," Cat said. "If I hadn't told Todd I wouldn't go out with him, he wouldn't have told the guys to vote for Marla."

"Me, too," Becka said. "I mean, I never considered the MacPhersons as a family for Michelle. But I *did* introduce her to them. So I guess I kept my promise, too."

Ben's forehead puckered. He shook his head wearily, frowned, and sat down.

141

"Now, Ben, don't worry about it," Annie said. "The girls know what they did."

"But have they learned anything from this?" Ben asked. He turned to his daughters. "Look, I'm glad everything's worked out for the best. But let's not have any more foolish promises. Try not to get yourselves into these kinds of situations again. Don't take on things you can't handle, or bite off more than you can chew. Okay?"

Becka, Josie, and Cat exchanged looks. Becka could tell they were all thinking the same thing. It was irresistible. With solemn faces, they all raised their right hands and spoke in unison.

"We promise." Then they dissolved in laughter at the look on Ben's face.